NO SMOKE

Also by Hugh Collins

Autobiography of a Murderer
Walking Away

NO SMOKE

Hugh Collins

CANONGATE

To my wife, Caroline, for the title and endless coffees —
thank you for everything, my wee darlin
— what a find.

First published in Great Britain in 2001 by Canongate Crime,
an imprint of Canongate Books Ltd, 14 High Street,
Edinburgh EH1 1TE

This edition published in the United States of America
and Cananda in 2002 by Canongate Books

10 9 8 7 6 5 4 3 2 1

British Library Cataloguing-in-Publication Data
A catalogue record for this book is available on
request from the British Library

ISBN 1 84195 116 1

Typeset by Palimpsest Book Production Limited,
Polmont, Stirlingshire
Printed and bound in Finland by
WS Bookwell

www.canongate.net

Glossary

ach	oh	ey	of (or he)
am	I'm	en	then
a	I	es	he's (or his)
al	I'll	eny	any
aw	all		
aye	yes	fur	for
auld	old	fun it	found it
aff	off	fitprints	footprints
aboot	about	frontey	front of
		fae	from
bampots	halfwits		
boays	boys	gonny	going to
battur	batter, to beat up	goan	go and
		goat	got
		gaun	going
canny	can't		
coodny	couldn't	huv	have
coonter	counter	haud	hold
		hullawrer	hello there
dae	do	heid	head
daen	doing	hauf	half
doon	down	hur	her
disnae	doesn't		
do'ra	do the	int	isn't
dint	didn't	isnae	is not
dinnit	doesn't it		
didny	didn't	jist	just
		jaikits	jackets

kin	can	*wan*	one
ken	know	*wanty*	want to
		wi	with
laddie	lad	*wull*	we'll
		wullny	will not
ma	my	*wis*	was
minit	minute	*weans*	children
mer	more	*wers*	where's
		wee	small
noa	not or (won't)	*wid*	would
naw	no	*wurkin*	working
noo	now	*wintit*	wasn't it
nae borra	no bother	*wrang*	wrong
		widda	would I (or would have)
oors	ours		
oot	out	*wit*	what
		witsat	what's that
pera	pair of	*wullny*	will not
		widnae	would not
real yin	right one (fool)		
		ye	you
shoodny	shouldn't	*yersel*	yourself
shoap	shop	*yin*	one
snecked up	locked up	*yev*	you've
soaks	socks	*yer*	your
swallyin	swallowing	*ye's*	you (plural)
tipple	get wise to	*ur*	are
thur	they're (or there)	*urra*	other
		um	him
tae	too		
twinty	twenty		
ukarenr	are		

Acknowledgements

Jamie, David, Karen, Stan, Sheila, Jim and all at Canongate. Special thanks to Alan Muir for endurance and support. Brian McEwan and Grace. Albert Faulds, Neil Murray and the people of the Garngad. Special thanks to Kevin Williamson. Anyone I owe money to – thanks, don't look for me just yet . . .

Part One

'Ur ye feelin lucky?'

The invisible is a trick; criminal non-violent activity, involving observation, speed and perfect timing. The basic requirement is confidence. Only two fundamental elements are necessary – an object and an escape route. Targeting prey is random. They are a catch on the end of a line. Caught – in any place, at any time. The main ingredient is greed. The rest is easy – watch.

Chapter One

BUCHANAN STREET, GLASGOW. July 1976. The heat is melting the tar on the road. Specks of grit melt into rubber as car tyres drag through the midday traffic. The three men hanging around outside the betting shop door are hot too. They are sweating in silence. The agitation they feel has nothing to do with the weather. They are waiting; they have been, for over two hours.

Barney, the older of the group, shifts, a motion barely noticeable to the mindless faces passing by, but enough to rouse the immediate attention of his associates. He hands his jacket to the youngest of the men – 'Here, Skud, haud this. This shoodny take too long. Thur there, jist across the road. There see thum, they two Pakis? That's thum. Lookit thum eh. Greedy bastards. Fuckin loaded tae.'

Pretending not to have noticed them, he continues with his softly spoken diatribe into the racing section of the newspaper he's holding – 'Jake, you stay beside the van, an mind, let thum see they car keys. Skud, you stay inside. They think am wurkin in the bettin shoap. Right en. In an oot. Canny go wrang.'

Jake, leaning against the van, gives a nod. Skud fades into the doorway, hidden from sight – 'Luck, Barney,' he whispers. Everything is in position. Jake spits phlegm onto the pavement. He watches the mucus sizzling – 'Black bastards,' he mutters.

Barney, looking up from the racing section, folds it up neatly into a pocket, and walks casually across the busy road. The two men are standing at the side of a car. Barney believes it to be theirs, but the car had, in fact, been parked only moments before they had arrived.

The driver of the car, a male, and a male passenger had both walked, unnoticed, into the Yellow Bird Café.

Barney eyes up his two men. He suspects that they will have a shop somewhere. One of those shops that sells cheap goods, mostly stolen in bulk. He doesn't mind at all, as long as they buy *his* goods. The thought appeals to his warped sense of humour. He thinks they're a tipple; hands in pockets, the shifting around and sideways glances, always watching over their shoulders. No wonder cops can always spot criminals when they are grafting with straight pegs – straight pegs are always nervous.

Little does he know how straight the two men are – how nervous indeed.

He'd met one of them the day before, in the betting shop. The guy thought he worked there – it was the pencil stub, sat snugly behind his ear, must have been that.

Saab nudges his younger brother, Rashid – 'Okay, Ra. Leave the talkin tae me. That's him there, crossin over, in the white shirt,' he whispers.

He feels slightly nervous. This is a first. He has never been involved in anything at all criminal – until now. The butterflies in his stomach. Would this man see through their act? These had to be serious criminals, after all, but would they recognise the phoney accents? He had doubted this, and put the hesitancy down to nerves alone. No, their plan had to succeed. Sanji, the eldest brother, conveniently absent, had thought it all through. Stick to the script, and nothing could go wrong, he'd told them. Still, Saab was shitting himself. This had started off as a lark

– they didn't need money. Sanji and his mother had invested well with their inheritance, a widow's army pension for life. Not much mind you, but with some common sense, and a wee bit of hardship, it had been enough to get started with a new life.

God. What would his father think?

Rashid looks beyond the figure coming toward them – 'Saab. Wait. Who's that guy? Thought thur wis supposed tae be jist twoey thum? A guy's hidin inside that doorway at the bettin shop. Al watch, jist incase it's a rip aff. Ye never know. These guys wid rob thur grannies. Ye really suit that turban by the way,' he giggles.

Saab's feeling tense, but he tries to look composed for his brother. He grins broadly, wagging his head, like a character from an old post-war colonial film – 'Mr Gungadin of India. I lie down. I carry water for great sirrr!' he whispers in a mock stereotypical accent – 'Goodness gracious me!'

Mahatma Gandhi and Gungadin had become blurred into one figure, fictionalised by British film versions of historical events, both in India and Pakistan. Films starring the blue-eyed, monarchic gentleman his-self, His Englishness – Sir David Niven.

Saab, in his absence of cultural education, believed both countries to be one and the same place. A perception the brothers had formed through the predominantly white Western media. Money, too, had induced laziness in the two younger boys. They had no need to look beyond their immediate means, no need to find out more about their family background.

Having been born and bred in Glasgow, they thought 'white'. How could they think anything else? They hadn't been brainwashed so much as whitewashed. They had a tan. So what? Colour had little to do with it. The climate in Scotland fed hatred of difference – colour or no colour.

Scots hated the English. They hated them too. They didn't know why, they just hated them. Had they known their history, they might have thought differently about making fun of the language of their forefathers. The dialect they spoke in today had itself had a facelift. A language, subjugated, and oppressed by the Queen's English. Indeed, it had been a criminal offence to speak one's native tongue in one's country. Had they probed they would have discovered that dialects had been all but obliterated from the dictionary of Standard English – Oh Aye – Abliteratcd so it wis.

Had they thought at all they might not have been here in the first place.

Jamaicans, African-Americans – they were black people. Saab, and his brother? No, they were Glaswegian. Pure by their very dialect. Deep down, they were white. Hadn't their father fought for his country? Saab and Rashid had no concept of the world outside Maryhill Road, Glasgow. They were, however, about to experience a colour-conscious awakening. The harsh reality of such a world was about to tear open their hearts. They were about to be devoured by predators, subjects of the butcher's bloody apron.

Saab walks around the car to greet the white meat stepping onto the pavement. The turban loosens slightly from the excessive wagging. Fuck, not now, he thinks. He adjusts the crimson silk curtain, borrowed from his mother that morning – 'Misterrr Barnee! Good day to you, sirrr! This my brother. Rashid! Say hello to my close friend Misterrr Barnee. Fine man indeed,' he grins stupidly.

Rashid's handsome head bows; he flashes brilliant white

teeth – 'I very pleased meet the very great Misterrr Barnee!' he smiles.

Barney takes in the sandals, and bare feet. Fuck me, he thinks. Darkies. Think they'd buy shoes, the cunts. He brushes the proffered hand – 'Hullawrer, Hashheid. How ye daen, son?' he grunts.

Skud remains hidden inside the front door of the bookies with the jackets, but he can see what's happening – 'Think Barney'll pull it aff, Jake?' he asks.

Jake, still leaning against the old transit van parked a few feet from the bookies, looks towards the men. He's throwing the bunch of keys up and down, snatching at them in mid air – 'Well, if eny cunt kin, it's Barney. Skud, don't let these two bampots see ye. They might tipple. They'll be acroass eny minit, so jist get ready tae head fur the back door.'

Barney's boozed-up face is like raw square sausage in the glaring sunlight. His head looks like a lump of granite, like a grotesque sculpture forced down onto the neck of a molten mass of undefined form. He looks pulverised, pulled down by gravity. The kiddie's bright-red anorak he has under his arm clashes with the drabness of his appearance. He'd stolen it earlier that day, stolen it from a pram sitting by a toy shop, in Sauchiehall Street. He'd lifted the jacket, almost in automatic response. His single thought being the best way to capitalise on its value. Most people walking through a city paid little attention to detail. Barney saw opportunity on every corner. He spent the day perpetually scavenging, tirelessly following a population, ceaselessly waiting, watching for its guard to drop. This observation had kept him alive, but there had to be famine, periods of hunger, driving him to desperation. Scotland's harsh climate often affected the pickings. A bad winter could often diminish the population's desire to go out, leaving him few options for survival. These things happened, they were an occupational hazard, so he'd simply crash in a shop window – and wait for the police to arrive. Porridge was a sustenance. A closed environment reduced the scale of the opportunities. Jails always had at least one halfwit per hall – A B C D E. That's five possibilities. A first offender who doesn't smoke? That's a dream come true.

Barney had spent most of his sixty-odd years doing regular short stints, or 'Jakeys', in jail. Probably this is what had preserved him from alcoholism, and an early death. He was a conman; conning was his speciality. Indiscriminate by definition, anyone was a fair target; there was no exception, no sense at racial inequality. Black, white, yellow, or red – he'd take them. Dog eat dog. Such was his simplistic philosophy to life.

Skud knew this from personal experience – Barney'd conned him after all. Indeed, it was how they had met each other in the first place. Back in 1967. They had been waiting together, down in the holding cells of the Sheriff Court, Ingram Street, Glasgow.

Skud had been done for breach of the peace, and being in possession of an offensive weapon – a hatchet. Barney? Who knows; a scam no doubt. He'd been entertaining the captive audience of the small auditorium with tales. The older men waiting to go upstairs to court had heard it all before, they merely looked on cynically, threatening physical violence with a glance. These hardened types knew the routine of court cells, the build-up of heat after a few hours, the stench of drink and sweat, the banging and shouting. They had acclimatised themselves, had developed tolerance through their experiences. They rarely spoke, they never sat on the steel bench, *never* begged the turnkeys for cigarettes, for mugs of water, or for the time. They insulated themselves from the others through indifference. Their brooding silence dampened any notions of gregarious questions. Every cell is occupied with people who want to know what's going to happen to them. This inevitably brings them together – 'What are you in for mate?' is the first question always asked. What lies behind the question is another question, the real question – 'What will happen to me, mate?'

No, those silent types are never asked. They simply lean against the steel walls of the tin cans considered as cells, moving only to relieve the cramp of standing on one leg for a few hours to change to the other foot.

Then there were those kind who were prepared to listen, indeed desperate to listen to the cell authority, the figure who knew everything about courts – the legal expert. The figure who would tell them what they wanted so much to hear – 'You Will Get Bail'. Barney had been the figure presenting such a voice that day – the cell's expert on law; he had been due to appear first before Sheriff Bain – AKA 'Santa Claus'. A man renowned for leniency, or as the case may be, complete lunacy. Nevertheless, Sheriff Bain had his moments of fury. He could be unpredictable, especially when the parade of faces became all too familiar. And yes, Barney was one of those faces. A face most likely to trigger off a bad day, particularly for those hoping to get bail. Bain knew him, knew him very well, but for those in the cell, those first-offender ears – they had no idea what might happen. They could only guess, and so they listened, hoping to hear what they wanted to hear – 'You Will Get Bail'.

Skud, too, had been one of those listeners, listening to that authority, that legal expert, hanging onto every word as the expert walked up and down. Barefoot. Barney had no shoes, but still those jaws had hung open, those gaping mouths, silent in the presence of this authority, of someone who knew; here was someone who had been down that road before.

No sane man would have listened to such a figure, however, this had to be more of a question about the desperation of a situation than the sanity of the characters snared by a network of circumstancial misfortunes. 'What if?' echoed around the cell's mostly dehydrated brains.

Skud had made that fatal mistake of listening, of seeking counsel – 'Eh, dae ye think al get a jail sentence if a plead guilty, mister?' he'd asked.

Barney, feigning interest with the practiced furrowed brow of a barrister, had stared in earnest, but not at the floor. Pretending to be listening, nodding in sympathy, he saw the shoes. That they were on feet made not the slightest bit of difference. He needed shoes. The boy, an obvious halfwit, was young – he would survive. Barney frowned. Size eight? A size seven? Two pairs of socks and they'll fit no bother. The boy doesn't know what day it is. Look at him. All skin and bone. A good dinner he needs. The jail would be the best thing for him. Fatten him up a bit. A decent bowl of porridge. He had thought about it long enough – 'Listen. Plead guilty, son. Ye'll get a fine. It's Santa up there the day. He'll never send ye tae the jail. Noa fur a breach,' he'd said.

Skud had fallen before the power of this man's obvious authority, he had heard those words he wanted to hear, felt the sincerety behind those words. He had decided what to do, but just to be certain, he'd asked – 'Ur ye sure, mistur?' Barney hadn't been about to dash the hopes of this young man. No. What would have been the point? No, Skud needed reassured. Barney needed shoes. The balance of necessity=exchange=hope.

The equilibrium of cell life=desperation.

Barney, the provider of hope, had provideth – 'Naw, plead guilty, son, ye'll walk. Auld Santa hates liars, jails thum. Ye'll walk, believe me, son,' he'd said.

Skud had loved being called son. The term had melted whatever resistance may have been left, or for that matter, existed in the first place. Few philosophical debates had ever occured within the realm of this young man's head. He had been functioning for most of his life on a purely emotional level, lurching from moment to moment without making any single connection in between. A short life had become a series of totally unrelated events, a blur of impulsive activity, shaped by mindless encounters – and a one way ticket to prison.

Barney, having tapped into the boy's disintegrated fabric had then taken him squarely by the shoulders, looked him straight in the eye, and promised, almost tearfully, that a friendship had been forged – 'Look, son. Al noa get bail. If ye come back doon, al be here, so don't you worry, okay?' He grins, winking reassuringly – Am Yer Pal.

Skud had felt the warmth of the arm around his shoulder as they walked up and down the cell together He'd felt he had found a person he could trust, for the first time he'd felt a connection, this deeply powerful bond – like a father and son, almost. And so, it had been an inevitable fact that he would lose something – his shoes.

When Barney had made his request to borrow the lad's shoes, Skud hadn't been able to get them off quick enough – 'Listen, son. Dae ye wanty dae me a favour? Kin ye lend me yer shoes? Jist tae a come back doon? A don't want tae go up in frontey aw they coppers in ma bare feet. Aye, the bastards took ma shoes fur fitprints last night.' He had whispered to the boy – 'Thur tryin tae dae me fur blown a safe last week. Ten grand the guys took. Me? C'mon son, dae a look like a safe blower?' he'd asked, the eyebrows raised, the beady twinkling eyes, and that rascal's grin.

Skud had been stunned – Jesus. Barney's modesty hadn't fooled him. No, he'd been too wide for that. A safe blower? Fuck. Wait till he tells the boys! A safe blower! He'd pulled the shoes off without question – 'Naw, honest, here man. Ye sure they fit ye okay? Dae ye want ma soaks? Naw, honest, dae they fit ye okay?' he'd insisted. Barney, as he knew he would, did get bail, leaving the shoeless wonder to appear in court, bearing a bewildered look on his face, and barefoot – 'Wers that auld guy? Es got ma fuckin shoes.'

The Sheriff had eyed him up and down as he stood in the dock; his tee shirt torn and bloodied from the struggle with the police when he'd been arrested. His long, hippie hairstyle he'd tied back in a ponytail to look presentable – but those bare feet?

Skud heard the sniggers from the public gallery when the judge asked – 'What do we have here then? A wild Indian? An Apache, perhaps? What were you doing walking the streets with a hatchet, young man?'

Skud mumbled – 'A fun it, yer majesty.'

Possibly Sheriff Bain's haemorrhoids had been bothering him. It may well have been the tomahawk, glinting menacingly on the table. Who knows? Barney had been right about one thing though – he didn't like liars. Santa banged the gavel – 'You found it, did you? Indeed! Well, maybe a spell in a reservation may help you find your senses, young man. Six months' imprisonment! Next!'

Skud, the young brave, had lost his freedom for six months – his shoes, forever.

He didn't see Barney again for a time, almost two years in fact – about '69. Old Bertie O'Hara, Skud's father, had been with the old rogue on that very day. They had been preying on an old woman carrying too many bags. Skud had spotted them tailing the woman, waiting to pounce – when he recognised Barney. He had been about to dig him up, but before he had been able to form a line of attack, he had been cut down, yet again, by that same patter – 'Skud! How ye daen, young yin? Witsat? Yer kiddin me on! Yer boay? Aw Bertie, es a good yin. Skud, here son, there's a cuppla quid son. Goan get yersel sweeties, son.' All said without so much as a blush.

Skud had been twenty-six years of age at the time. The couple of quid had been just that – two pounds. Still, Barney was an earner, a grafter, a man with unique opportunistic qualities, skilled in shoplifting, burglary – a conman. He might learn something from this man, he'd thought. Well, let's face it, he had learned a lesson in the process of his previous encounter – never trust a man in a cell, especially in his bare feet, and bearing a frown.

Now, some seven years hence, he was learning the art of the invisible, listening still, to that same voice.

Auld Barney. There he was, sixty-seven years old, and still working on the street, still watching for the slightest shift in the herd, still watching, waiting for its guard to drop for a single moment, for one inconsistency in crowd motion – and he'd take them. Back in the here and now, back in the sweltering heat. Two such victims were about to be just that – cut down.

Jake's showing out – 'Skud, here, listen. Thur swallyin it. Barney's pointin tae the van. Thur comin o'er so get ready tae move,' he whispers.

Barney had handed one of them the anorak. The taller of the two men appeared to be examining it for flaws. He was smiling at his partner. Then, after a moment, they both began smiling. Yes, they would all be shaking hands very soon.

Saab looked at the red anorak, kneading the fabric between thumb and forefinger. An obvious expert in cheap bri-nylon – 'Ahh, Misterrr Barnee. Fine qualitee mateerial. Oh, yes sirrr!' he said excitedly in the exaggerated accent. He fingered his black beard – 'Is jackets all red, sirrr? Oh, no, no, sirrr! This is not any problem for Saab. No, it is very fine indeed,' he assured the man. 'How many did you say, sirrr?'

Barney scents a kill. Yes. He's swallowed it. He thumbs over his shoulder with a dirty gnarled stub, indicating the van parked across the street – 'Twinty-four gross, Shabby. In the van, ootside the bettin shoap. Ye goat the muney wi ye? C'mon, wull aw cross o'er an huv a look then,' he suggests.

Twenty-four gross? At a pound each? Saab could quadruple that price. Greed overtakes common sense.

'Skud, get ready. Thur in,' signals Jake.

Barney whispers to Saab out the side of his face as the three of them walk towards the parked van – 'Shabby. Guy wi the blue jaikit. He's haudin the keys, bran new, but nuts. Well ey disnae like your mob. Pakis, darkies an that. Naw es bran new, jist disnae talk so don't panic. A fuckin nutter,' he says assuringly, ensuring a speedy deal.

Barney and the two men find their way through traffic and reach the van. The anorak vanishes, sunk inside a baggy silk kaftan.

Saab and Rashid's eyes meet in a glance filled with recognition. A pure bampot, they silently agree. Saab is reassuring – 'Ohh, fine Misterrr Barnee. Rashid speak verr little Scoatteesh. He have money in pocket so no worry, my close friend,' he says, grinning stupidly, steepled fingers touching his bearded chin. This fuckin turban, man.

He's taking in the traffic lights. Easy now. Don't fuck this up. As soon as these lights turn green, get the keys an GO GO GO. Saab then spots a scarred face trying hard to conceal its presence. Here. Rashid's right enough. That's definitely backup. He'll have a knife. Jesus, look at that scar down his face!

Skud's torn face pulls further back into the doorway but he can hear them talking. Jake's swinging the bunch of keys. He's saying nothing while the others reach an agreement about the price for the jackets in the van.

Barney sounds in a generous mood – 'Right noo. Thurs twenty-four gross. Thur aw in boxes by the way, except the wan yev already goat. So lets see.' The frown is a remarkable feature of his method in mental arithmetic – 'At a nicker an anarak, that's wit? Three-an-a-hauf grand. Tell ye wit, call it three grand, okay? Right then. C'mon. Av got tae get back behind that coonter.'

Skud can't believe his ears. Three grand?

Barney pushes the deal through now, finalising the transaction with them. Jake then plays his part. He throws the keys to Barney, then walks straight through to a back door, inside the betting shop – 'Am stickin a bet oan. Catch ye in there, aul yin.' Black hate reaches out from his eyes, but the brothers pay no attention to the flow of resentment. Why should they? This is Glasgow, and they're Glaswegian. They have eyes only for the keys, and those boxes full of red anoraks.

Barney too is taking in the traffic. Right, now. Nice and easy. As soon as these lights change it's right through that fucking door. Three grand. A cake walk. Right. Just watch for the wee green man. The timing's perfect. The bundle of bank notes become a blur of keys and notes changing hands to the theme tune of the flashing green man, as he signals – WALK NOW. WALK NOW. WALK NOW.

Barney has the money in his tail. He's talking them down, keeping them sweet – 'Noo leave the van here when ye's finish unloadin the jaikits. Leave the keys under a seat, the driver's lifts up. Right, thurs weans shoes comin in next week, but keep this quiet cuz a don't want eny cunt tae know av goat a contact in that factory. Ma boss hearsa whisper ey this an am fur a heavy bowla purridge.'

Saab has the keys secured. Yeeees. Easy, Saab, e-aasy. He's seriously wagging now, but stays cool – 'Misterrr Barnee. My close friend. It is indeed good to do'ra business with you. You come to shop. Saab will make you a vunderful curree, yes? Vunderful hot vindaloo for close friend Misterrr Barnee. Yes indeed. Oh my goodness gracious me. Look at the time.'

Barney's antennae immediately lock onto the silver Rolex watch. *Bastard*. This cunt's loaded. They would've jumped at twice the price, the greedy bastards. Ach well. He beams – 'Okay, Shabby! Good daen bisness wi ye, son! Mind. Thurs shoes in next week. A finish work in the bettin shoap at half two so say three, here? Fine then,' he says, waving.

Skud has the exit door open as the Pakistani guy thanks Barney – 'We'll leave de keys under de seat, Misterrr Barnee. You no worree about van. Saab honest man, like you my close friend!' he calls after him.

Barney and Jake come bursting through the fire exit – 'C'mon Skud. Geez that jaikit. Let's get tae fuck afore they two bampots tipple the van's noa oors. Widda tell ye's eh? Black greedy bastards!'

Saab's relieved to be rid of the turban – 'Wit aboot that then, Ra? Twinty-four gross ey these wee jaikits eh? Right, you phone Sanji. Tell um the score. Then we kin take the van up tae es new shop in Maryhill Road. Wit aboot that accent, eh? Misterrr Barnee!' Rashid pats the van – 'Wit aboot this when it's emptied?' he asks.

Saab looks the van over – 'Ach, dump it in a canal ur jist leave it in a lane. We better avoid that bookie's fur awhile. They cunts won't be too pleased when they tipple. Aye, twinty-four gross, eh. Right, al see ye when ye get back. They thought that wis oor car across the road as well! The fuckin bampots, eh. Jesus. That wis so easy, wint it? Sanji wis right aboot that money lookin the part.' The danger is infectious, addictive – 'That wis a cake walk, man,' he says, amazed the deal had gone down with such ease – 'A pure cake walk.'

They're both laughing, looking across the street at the car, but there's little time for an inspection. Saab pushes his brother firmly – 'Right, c'mon. Get movin. Al drive when ye get back. Hope the gear's in plastic wrappers, easier tae unload. Sanji said punters love thur gear in cellaphane, makes it look dearer,' he says. 'Right, hurry up. Al be in the van.'

Barney and the others have run down a few lanes, and emerge at the bottom of Union Street. They jump a taxi to find a quiet pub to divide the money – 'Eh. The Woodside Inn, driver. Aye, jist afore ye hit Maryhill Road.'

Chapter Two

THE WOODSIDE IS near enough empty when they arrive. The few pints of heavy, spread sparsely along the length of the bar, sit snugly under a row of two-day growths and a cloud of spiralling smoke. Heads, propped up by elbows and long bony fingers, glance in their direction as they reach the bar. Other faces take a peek, but are mostly engrossed in the racing sections of newspapers. Their screwed-up eyes, peering from the side to dodge the clouds of smoke from fags, search forlornly for that winning horse. Every aspect of these figures seems askew, undernourished, dilapidated, and yet – the sheer elegance of these men.

'How ye doin, Barney,' one states without so much as a glance in any one direction.

'How ye doin, Tony. A pint?' Barney enquires, making sure he gets the opportunity to flash the wad. Well, let's face it. What would be the point if you couldn't show off. You flashed the cash, dug up a bird – blow it. These are the widos, the gemmies, game boys: by dawn they won't have a penny. They'll tour Glasgow, hit the bevvie, unharness some heavy swaggers as they take the floor – they'll have had a ball. Stars of their own private film, the impromptu premiere is now in full flow.

Tony smiles wryly, acknowledging the bundle – 'Nae borra, auld yin. A pinta heavy, an a wee yin. Get a turn at the bingo?' he grins, before hunching back inside the racing section.

Barney has to meet some people, he says, as they hit the

lounge – 'There ye go lads, a grand each. Am jist daen a wee message an al be back. Better avoid that bettin shop in Buchanan Street. Aye, they thought a worked there. Pera fuckin halfwits the twoey thum. Told ye dint a? Canny go wrang,' he laughs. He ponders for a moment. The beady eyes twinkling gleefully – 'Ye's know eny cunt lookin fur cheap anaraks! Ha ha ha!' He pulls a fifty-pound note, deliberately drags it from the bundle, purely for the benefit of the big-busted blonde behind the bar, with a now surprised look on her face – 'Two lagers fur the boays there.' He winks at her, licking his lips obscenely – 'Jist keep the change. Al noa be long, darlin.'

Barney's appearance contradicts his apparent affluence yet somehow confirms an old theory, that the impoverished mind has no economic understanding of currency. This default of the mind has been known to wreck the best of plans, indeed, is more often than not the very cause of capture. It's often brought on by peripheral blindness, and sudden, momentary states of euphoria. Either that, or they just don't give a fuck for the concept of long-term planning. It's all the same to them – just depends who's watching at the time.

The big blonde looks him over. She just happens to be the manageress of the boozer, just happens to be an ex-police woman at that. She reaches for the telephone with not so much as a word of thanks. Forty-odd quid's quite a tip – 'Hello. Put me straight through to DS Tom Forest. Yes, Karen Murray. Okay. The desk sergeant then,' says the blonde bombshell, from behind the bar – 'S'fine, al wait, thanks.'

Karen dismisses the kiss blown in her direction. She gags at the idea of that dried, cracked slit on her mouth, snaking her tongue. She shudders as it disappears through the door – 'Desk Sergeant? Is that you Boab? Oh, fine. Listen . . .'

Barney hasn't made the door yet, and already his description has been relayed down a telephone line – directly linked to the Glasgow Central Police Station. The distance, no more than a few minutes from the bar, maybe even seconds by van, travelling say at sixty-miles-per-hour – face down, in handcuffs.

Barney's completely unaware of what fate has in store as he saunters, whistling, down Woodside Road. Fuck me, he thinks. She's bursting for it. The tits on it. Pushing them out too, the big cow. Thinks he didn't notice. Too wide for her. Oh, he's right in there later. Big fucking darling. That forty quid should cover it. Get shot of Jake and Skud as soon as they get drunk. Get her up to a house somewhere. Just the two of them. Give her a good sausaging, the big cow – 'Aye. Give me sunshine! Give me spring!' he hums heartily to himself.

Skud and Jake are locked in deep discussion when the barmaid reappears with free lagers – 'S'on the house, boys. Who's yer pal? Barney? Must be loaded. Gave me a tip, forty quid. Wish aw ma customers were like him,' she says innocently.

Jake's mood has been shifted by an altered state of wealth, his sensibilities have been seduced by the bundle burning the hole in his pocket. He hits the blonde with a flim, which she sticks down her barely concealed front – 'Ohhh. Thanks, handsome. Shout if ye need anythin else,' she smiles, all lips and tongue. Jake watches her wiggle off. She's bursting fur it. Check that fucking arse, man. Wiggling away there. He's up that the night. Chase Barney, and this bampot. Get her up to a gaff somewhere, and give her the tajjer. Get her drunk first, and then give her a right good tajjerin, the big cow.

Skud swallows half a pint of lager before resuming his

private reverie. Whether to buy his bird a leather coat, or not? Jake'll know. Jake knows everything – 'Listen, Dawn wants a leathur coat. Dae ye think a shood buy ur wan?' he asks.

Jake buying women anything? He has never so much as smiled without some ulterior motive. Smile? Who wants to do that for nothing? Does Clint Eastwood smile? Jake looks thoughtful, before delivering his bland reply – 'Nah.'

Skud considers the logic behind the gesture – 'Keeps hur mooth shut, dinnit? A saw a good wan the urra day, full-length, two hunner quid,' he continues. Two hundred quid? On a woman? Reality penetrates fantasy. Jake's right – 'Nah Jake, fuck it. Yer right. Two hunner quid oan that cow?'

He lumbers on with another idea – 'Here! Fancy the pictures? Eh? *Durty Harry*'s oan at the Odeon. Fancy? Take a bottla wine in wi us?' That they have seen the film half-a-dozen times doesn't dampen his enthusiasm to see it again – 'Clint Eastwood's brulliant int ey? Mind that bit wi the Magnum?'

Jake interjects, displaying his supreme precision and an acute accuracy of memory for such significant events – 'Aye, that black cunt coodny remember if it is wis five ur six bullits the big yin hud fired. A widda emptied the gun intae that black bastard's heid,' he says, remembering.

Dirty Harry? Not a bad idea, thinks Jake – 'Right, a cuppla pints. See Barney, an then we kin head up the toon. Get a taxi, incase they two Pakis coppered us up,' he says, remembering another black face – 'Here, didye check the fat yin wi the turban? Probably a fuckin towel eh. A wis dyin tae battur the two ey thum. Black bastards. A fuckin hate the lot ey thum.'

Speaking of which. In another not too far distant part of the city. Two detectives had begun questioning a man of dark persuasion. The exchange concerned a stolen van, dumped outside a betting shop, two days earlier – 'Excuse me. This your van?' asked the taller of two detectives.

Saab had jerked away from the van the minute he'd felt the hand on his left shoulder; not quickly enough, unfortunately. The dangling keys flickering in the intensely glaring sunshine had also attracted his fingerprints. He'd been, as they say, caught red-handed – 'Eh? Wit? No! No! It's not my van! Naw, honest! I've never seen it before in my life! Honest, eh sir, oafficur,' he exclaims.

A six-foot frame bends slightly to hear the jabbering mouth before him – 'Are ye sure ey that? We've been watching ye. Fae the car across the road fur the past half hoor. Wit's inside this van then, laddie?' the frame persists.

Saab's brain, somehow, is unable to form a single train of thought. His head's become fully occupied with images of boxes, containing twenty-four gross of jackets, wee red anorak jackets. Fuck No! Red Anoraks! Fuck No! Please! No! Pleeaaase! The red nylon fabric under his father's old kaftan has suddenly become extremely hot, to far greater degrees than the pungent emissions escaping from his fluttering anal passage – *phhhhuuutttt. Phhhhrrrtttttt. Phhhhhhrrrrr-chhhhhttttt.*

The detective has become aware of the strong odour polluting the atmosphere – 'Aw, Jesus Christ. Wis that you?' The six-foot frame re-erects itself to a higher altitude, to escape poisoning from the toxic waste – 'Right, Hector. Name an address,' he shouts down with a cold, malignant glare, matched by an even more menacing tone.

Saab can barely contain his terror. He has never set foot inside a police station in his short twenty-six years on this planet. His mouth feels dry, deprived of saliva, his legs too are trembling, uncontrollably. The dark patch spreading across his silk pantaloon trousers is evaporating into steam in the hot climate – 'Honest boss. They anoraks in the van urny mine. Honest, a bought thum aff a guy. Please believe me,' he pleads. The fright has loosened his tongue. The dialect of his countrymen doesn't seem that funny now as he faces the detective – 'Honest surr they're noa mine! A bought thum aff these guys. Wanney thum's got this big scar doon throo es eye! Hon-eest. A gave thum three grand! Wans called Barney!' he blabbers out.

When the other detective reappears from the back of the van he becomes even more confused. The detective's looking at him – 'Wit anoraks wid that be? It's empty. And where did you get three grand? Any receipts?' he asks, pulling out handcuffs – 'Eh?'

Saab's head is swooning – 'Whugh? The anoraks. A bought them off the guy. Thur a red plastic. Thur in the van ey said. Honest, sir, they told me. Aw pleease. Naaaaaw.'

The detective handcuffs his arms behind his back, pushing him toward the car across the road – 'Right, move. Your cumin wi us,' he grins.

Saab feels people staring; the antagonistic eyes of the whole street scorch his skin as furrowed brows bear down upon him. He hears murmurs about unemployment, and the black bastards who shouldn't even be here – 'Nae wunder white peepul canny get fuckin joabs, eh. These black bastards everywhere.'

He can't believe it as he's pushed into the car, the one parked at the kerb, outside The Yellow Bird Café – 'Right, mind yer heid. Noo shut the fuck up, son. Stoap the greetin,' orders the smaller detective – 'Take um tae the Central, Tam. A wish tae fuck ey wid shut up,' he sighs with resignation.

*   *   *

Rashid freaks when he sees the two police uniforms eyeing up the van – 'The co-pps? Where's Saab?' he wonders – 'Wit the fuck's happened?'

He pulls back into the lane, turns to bolt, but falls into a steady walk, staying close to the walls of the narrow lane; they don't see him, but they'll know, he thinks. They'll know that he was involved, his brother would tell them, he'll collapse and tell the cops everything.

'Sanji,' he hisses – 'A bettur tell um case the cops turn up at the shop. Oh, Jesus,' he laments – 'Him n es big ideas. A knew sumthin like this would happen. Ad a feelin aboot this fae the beginning.' – 'A knew it, we shood nevera got involved wi gangsturs.'

Saab's walling from the back seat is beginning to seriously irritate the detective – 'Aw, here, you!' shouts the detective.

WHACKKKKKKKKKK!

The back-hander has the desired effect. The unfortunate passenger is stunned into an immediate silence by the shock of the unexpected blow – 'That's yer last warnin. Noo am tellin ye,' he warns him. He winks to his partner – 'Any mer ey it an yer gaun straight tae Barlinnie. See how ye like the jail, eh? Might get rode up there wi some lifer. Dae ye fancy that, Hector?' he sneers vehemently.

Saab quietly replies – 'No, sir.' He squeezes his eyes shut, trying, with great difficulty, to be somewhere else, preferably with his family, at home, with his 'true' people. But home is here, home is Glasgow, and he is Scottish – and these are his people.

The detective glances at his partner, Tom – 'Here, you ridin that wee Anne? Naw? Av heard she takes it aw roads.

Some arse, eh? She looks sumthin else in that uniform,' he murmurs, feeling an erection coming on – 'You awright back there, Hector? Yer noa sayin much, eh? Dae ye know who we are by the way? Answer me. Cunt,' he snaps.

WHACKKKKKKKKKKK!

Saab recoils from the blow – 'Don't ignore me, ya fuckin real yin!' shouts the detective furiously – 'Paki bastards! Who dae ye think ye ur? Eh, ya black bastard? D'ye hear wit a said? We're the fuckin Untouchables!' he spits venomously.

WHACKKKKKKKKKKK!

WHACKKKKKKKKKKK!

Saab's terrified face is bleeding from the blows – 'Yes sir, am sorry, sir,' he stammers.

WHACKKKKKKKKKKK!

The detective's flushed face breaks into a sweat, his eyes shining – 'Aye. Heard me that time, eh? Aye, that's better. Jist don't get wide wi us son, okay.'

He turns to his partner – 'Think that wee Anne wid go fur a drink wi me, Tam? Aye? A widnae mind a good ride at that wee arse ey hurs. Huv legs like rubber by the time a wis finished eh. Right then big man, here we go. Get this bampot snecked up. Jesus! Burstin wi the fuckin horn here, big man.'

Saab flinches as the detective swings round – 'Noo wur noa gonny get any shite fae you ur wi? You jist make a statement and tell us aw aboot this three grand. Ye don't want another skelp in the mooth dae ye?' he grins, his flesh fully hardened, bursting, pushing against the restraints of his tightly bound underpants. He can feel the cord cutting up into his cheeks. A painful, but pleasurable sensation – 'Aw, Tam! Ye could hing yer coat oan this thing. Feel that, man!' he laughs, as his partner shies away, embarrassed.

Saab has been muted by the unpredictability of the detective. He's too afraid to reply, to even look at the uniformed sergeant at the desk as he's being booked at the police station – 'No sir. Av nuthing to say,' he says quietly, head bowed.

Tom removes the handcuffs – 'Theft, police assault, oh, and resistin arrest. Listen, kin you deal wi the personal property and things? Thanks, Boab. Jerry's havin a slash so al grab a wee cuppa tea. How's things anyway, Boab?' he asks.

Boab raises his eyebrows without looking up from the charge sheet – 'Ach, fairly quiet, Tom. This thing pissed itself?' he asks, smelling urine.

Tom notices the damp patch – 'Och, look at that. Shood behave thumselves then,' he replies, shaking his head.

Boab agrees – 'Al put him doon the stairs. Still swelterin ootside? Aye, well, suppose it might last a few mer days, so they say. Am takin the missus tae Cyprus. Right, Tom. Leave this yin wi me. That Big Karen left a message. Cuppla characters flashin cash up in the pub. Thinks the notes are duds,' he finishes, still without having looked up from the desk paraphernalia.

Tom heads for the canteen as the prisoner is booked – 'Right, yer name and address please,' requests the desk sergeant. He then drums a finger on the bloodied bartop.

'Remove your belt. And shoe laces. Empty your pockets onto the desk. Lets see noo. One turban – red. One Rolex watch. One silk, wit? Vest or a shirt? A kaftan? Oh, a see. One leather belt, black, with silver buckle.'

Boab looks at the kid's red anorak – 'Oh, and what's this? One red anorak? Have any children then?' he asks, with a certain tone, a tone reserved for paedophiles.

Saab's heart accelerates as he's steered to the fingerprint room. The florescent lights are blinding, but he recognises the battered swollen reflection in a tea urn – his face. A female police officer fingerprints him, leaving his soft white palms blackened with ink – 'Eh, there's some spirits in that bottle. There's a towel over there, but wash your hands in the sink first with soap,' she says, before returning him to the desk sergeant.

Auld Boab, transfixed still by the charge book, finally puts the pencil behind his ear and selects a huge key from the bunch hanging by his knee – 'Number three. A rubber mat wid be better, but we need the space. That's seven in number three aw the gither. Av a feelin it's gonny be a bizzy night. This weather. Right then, in ye go,' says the forty years of experience.

A chorus of frustrated anxiety greets the turnkey – 'Boss! Boss! Boss! Boss! Fuck!' CLANG – FUCKIN ARSHOLE! GEEZA MUG A WATER YA CUNT YE! FUCKIN COW!' Saab is now in the chamber of What If. There is barely room to stand in the tiny steel box, but he finds space next to the stinking stainless steel urinal. The six faces are a mixture of red watery eyes and sleekit glances filled with blind ire, but he presents a break, possibly hope, for a moment anyway – 'Any fags? Wit ye dun fur? Think ye'll get bail? Think al get bail?'

A figure with feather-cut ginger hair asks quietly – 'Ye okay, pal? Wer ye fae?'

Saab finds his voice – 'Am sorry, a don't smoke. Am fae Maryhill,' he replies, almost apologetically.

The feather-cut hair detects fear – 'Wit're ye dun fur?' he asks. The green polo neck sweater, the full-length leather coat, smell of gang mentality. That tight, wiry, muscular build spells trouble, but he seems quiet, confident – 'Johnny, by the way. A cum fae the Garngad. Maryhill? D'ye know Rab Carruthers? Usety run aboot wi that Maryhill Fleet mob?'

Saab accepts the handshake – 'Eh, Saab. Pleased tae meet ye. Eh, Rab Carrudars?'

Johnny's patient – 'Ye sure yer fae Maryhill?' the boxer-type face asks, with a slightly amused grin and raised eyebrows.

The grin elevates him above the fighting machine coolness he exudes. This is the cell authority, but this figure has immaculately polished shoes – platforms.

Saab notices that Johnny alone has the exclusive space to walk up and down the centre of the cell without any human obstacles – 'Here you, shift,' he commands – 'Gie the guy a seat.' He then expresses concern – 'Happened tae yer face, pal? Coppers? Sit doon before ye end up stinkin wi piss next tae that thing.'

Saab complies without question, but secretly worries that the evicted arse might take offence – 'Thanks Johnny, am okay. The cops gave me a right doin. Aye, said they're the Untouchables.'

Johnny smiles knowingly – 'Aye, the Untouchables eh. A broke wanney thur jaws up the toon. They used tae drive aboot in a blue van. We battured thum years ago, aye up in the George Hotel. Wrecked the fuckin place. Bampots. A wis runnin aboot the toon. Wanney the Shamrock. Heard ey thum? Naw? You *sure* yer fae Maryhill?' he again asks, mockingly.

He remains apart from the other cellmates, leaning against the wall – 'Here, ye wanta fag? Naw, yeı awright. Don't worry aboot any ey these cunts.' He nods to a guy – 'Here, you, shift.'

Saab's luck appeared to be changing – 'Aye, Johnny. The Shamrock? Av heard ey it. Were they a big gang?' he asks, innocently – 'Wur they fae this, this, eh Garineegad? That wit ye call it?' Johnny merely grins – 'Garineegad? Sounds like a hoat curry, fur fucksake.'

The Shamrock had been the first predominantly Catholic gang to emerge from an area known as the Garngad. The Gaelic dictionary defines *Garn* as meaning *rough ground*. *Gad* would have been referring to the burn which ran nearby – a burn no longer there these days. The Garngadhill had been one of many hills left after the Ice Age. At two-hundred-and-fifty-odd feet, it remained one of the most impressive glaciers in the city. Many Irish Catholic immigrants saw the area as home.

To the Shamrock – the Holy Ground.

Their Provisional IRA affiliation could be heard every Saturday. The Parkhead Jungle provided the platform. Irish rebel Songs could be heard for miles around – 'So-oljurs Ur We!' That Sinn Fein and the IRA were politically Marxist was just coincidental. They collected money, and fought Protestants. That was all that mattered to the Shamrock. They had become disintegrated to a degree by the hippie flower power explosions of drugs, peace and free love. This was no wallflower leaning against that steel panel, however – this was a *rough ground boy* through and through.

Saab begins to feel more secure. He confides in the authority – 'Aye, a dun a deal wi this auld guy, but somethin happened. Well, thur wis nae gear in the van, an noo the cops are chargin me wi stealin the van aswell. A guy called Barney.'

Johnny laughs – 'Barney? A wee guy, durty fair hair? Yer kiddin, a bookie? Barney Boone? Dae a know um? The whola Glesga knows Barney. Did ye gie um money?' he asks.

Saab's in too deep now to get clever – 'Well Johnny, it wis ma big bruther. Gave me three grand, but it's aw dummy muney, forgeries. Aye, Barney took the muney. Gave me a wee red anarak. Am dun fur that, an a polis assault tae. Dae ye think they'll let me oot oan bail?' he asks.

Johnny's finding the whole scenario hilarious – 'Barney bumped you, an you bumped him? Auld Barney, eh. At long last,' he laughs.

The cell door is opened. Jerry the detective is standing there – 'Right, Hector. C'mon. Time fur a wee blether,' he says.

He quickly scans the faces – 'You in fur, McGinty?'

Johnny barely moves – 'Naney your fuckin bizness, poof,' he replies.

Saab is stunned by this total disregard for the detective. No slapping? No punching? He feels the imprint of the three steel bars on his arse as he rises from the bench, but his battered face is more painful. He's terrified of this man. There's something about him, something not quite right – 'Right, sir. Right, sir,' he stammers.

Johnny's sneering smile is the last thing he sees as the cell door is slammed shut – 'A Shamrock punter, eh? Irish bastards,' the detective mutters to himself as he locks the door as forcefully as possible. He pushes his prisoner towards an interview room – 'A fuckin bampot. Noa like you, eh Hector?'

Saab's shuffling along, trying to hold up his trousers and walk with flapping shoes at the same time – 'Naw, sir. Naw, honest,' he quakes.

The interview room is empty when they arrive. Saab's pushed into a plastic chair and told to relax – 'Right noo. Here, dae ye want a fag? Naw? Okay then, but ye kin see, am a fair man. Noo a don't like tae get fucked aboot so let's make this easy, an ye kin go hame withoot any trouble.'

Home? Saabs heart floods tears, as brothers, family, familiarities, flash through brain cells. He's broken already, confused, and afraid – 'Yes, sir,' he weeps.

The detective gets straight to the point – 'Where's this three grand? Who's got it?' he asks quietly – 'Noo, you tell me who's got it an this'll disappear. Al huv a talk wi Tam. He disny like you by the way. Fae the Highlands. Hates darkies.'

He pauses for effect – 'Dae ye know that ye kin get two years for police assault alone? Well, you jist tell me the truth aboot the three grand. Oh, don't you worry aboot these bampots. Al sort that oot. This Barney. Does he have straw-coloured hair?'

Saab is getting deeper and deeper into a hole. The truth hurts, but kills too. He can't think of a way out of this without trouble either way – 'Yes sir, that's him. He's got the three grand, but eh, the mone—' he tries to explain.

WHACKKKKKKKKKKK!

Jerry loosens his tie. A film of sweat has formed on his forehead. His dick is hurting, bursting to be freed – 'Listen, av told ye. Nae shite. THE FUCKIN MONEY!'

Saab becomes a quivering mass of terror – 'Honest! A canny tell ye anythin else. Oh please don't hit me again, sir, ma jaws aw sore, sir,' he cries.

He's dragged to his feet. The detective's breathing heavily, gripping him by the throat until he can see stars and colours swimming before his eyes. His head hits the door's frame as his arms are twisted up his back and he's run down to the holding cells like some human battering ram. The hard body pressing him down onto the rubber mat is now panting in his ear – 'Am fuckin warnin ye . . .'

Saab can barely breathe from the writhing weight on top of him. He can hear a voice but it's becoming distant, faint. He is unable to resist the armlock. A fumbling, a fist, belt buckle loosening. He can feel these movements close against his buttocks. That tightening feeling around his neck. He can smell the leather belt in his nostrils. Then the pain as it is pulled – tighter, and tighter. He feels the blood burst through his eyes, before his life force fades, recedes into painless, nothingness – *Father, is that you? Is it really you, father?*, are the young man's final thoughts.

Upstairs, Tom's smiling – 'Okay, Boab. Jerry back? Al wait in the car park. We'll take a run o'er tae the Woodside. Aw, here ey comes noo. Where have ye been, man? Av been in the canteen for ages. Thought ye'd nipped that wee Anne? Right, let's head up tae the Woodside.'

Jerry's flushed face is smiling – 'Guess who wur lookin fur? Barney Boone. Aye, that Paki spilled es guts. Boab had put um in wi McGinty. Aye, so av put him in an empty cell. Think McGinty battured the poor cunt, looked in a mess, unconscious.'

He claps his hands together – 'Right, big man! Lets go! He told me everythin. Barney Boone eh. Jist leave him tae me,' he says.

On reaching the car he remarks – 'Fuck. Av dripped aw doon ma trooser leg. Lookit that. Need tae stick them in the cleaners noo.'

Tom had never been interested in the rough stuff. He had known for a long time that his partner had a temper, but you didn't rat on a collegue, not against criminals, they were the scum, not the cops. Those journalists should see the victims before they had a go at the police. They were the front line, facing dangerous situations. But no one was interested in that. No, it had always been the same – the poor criminals. They'd always had it easy. No, Jerry had been a good mate. The police force needed more men like him. So, he used his truncheon a lot. These thugs were using razors. They were scum. The force needed men like Jerry. They – the Untouchables – had smashed the gangs. Jerry waded in when he was needed. That's what mattered. A few grand going missing – so what? No, you never grassed a mate. Jerry was a mate. Big Tom would let him deal with this. He'd hoped they would be working together on the new drug squad team being formed. You needed someone you could trust. Someone who knew how to deal with this new menace on the streets. Barney Boone? Scum. Jerry would know what to do with him. Aye, leave it to him, he knew best. Anyway, Karen might even fancy a wee quickie later – 'Jerry, yer shirt's covered in ink. Oh, dear. Wit a mess. Karen might have a clean one behind the bar,' he blushes.

Jerry roars hysterically – 'Ya big real yin, Tommy! A knew ye wur ridin hur! Aye, kept that quiet, eh big man! Ach, good on ye, big yin. Och, nae problem. Al no say a word. Your Maureen wid hit the fuckin roof if she found oot ye wur pumpin big Karen. Here, between you an me noo. She take it up the arse? C'mon big yin. Dis she? She like it up the back?'

Tom's face is scarlet with embarrassment. He had hidden his shyness behind all that tall dark silent bullshit. Maureen, his wife, had never imagined for a moment that this huge shy man could have been capable of having affairs. Jerry, though, had been his partner for years, had seen more of him than his own wife – 'Aye, Jerry, well, a kin get carried away. The heat ey the moment. Ach, ye know wit a mean eh.'

Jerry is roaring, but the vision of his partner fucking this slag in the arse had stamped a permanent image on his brain, which was now swollen, and struggling once again to break free of the restrictive Y-fronts. All his underpants were too tight, but you had to protect your balls in a fight, didn't you? He slaps his partner's back – 'Big Tom, eh. Need tae keep an eye on you, big yin. The big Highlander, doon here shaggin aw oor wumin,' he roars.

His expression changes as an idea forms – 'Here, ye shood dae a blue movie. You an Karen. A wid dae it fur ye. Aw, don't be daft, be a good laugh. Dae ye honestly think a wid tell anybody in the station? Right, c'mon before they spend aw the money. Aye, big Karen eh,' he leers.

Chapter Three

THE WOODSIDE IS normally quite dark inside, but the explosion of light blinding the bar has nothing to do with the weather – 'Hullawrer, darlin!' exclaims a voice.

Karen is startled by the transformation walking through the doors of the pub – 'Told ye ad be back, darlin. Ma two boays still here? Right, three lagers, pronto, an you keep the rest fur yerself, darlin,' he suggests, again winking obscenely.

Barney saunters through to the lounge, patting down his straw-coloured hair, pressed to the skull. That centre parting could easily have been made by the sharp edge of a meat cleaver – there's not a hair out of place in that shed.

'Hullaw! Rer!' he exclaims, arms outstretched, a new camel coat draped over one and a businessman-type black brolly dangling from the other.

Those theories about the economic inadequacy of an impoverished soul are are being put to the test today, by the living embodiment itself – Barney.

Skud and Jake are halfway to paradise with lager – 'Jeez! Barney! Check the suit! A like the coat, auld yin! Fuckin hell, man! Musta cost a right few quid. Here, ye must be swelterin man. Thurs Brylcreem runnin doon yer face!' they laugh.

Barney's new red socks become exposed as he takes a seat, revealing a colour crisis against the black-and-white checkered, silverish zoot suit – 'Aye, eh? Widdae ye think then? Check these,' he says, bringing out a pair of silver-framed sunglasses – 'Am in disguise . . .'

He grins, balancing the glasses precariously on his flat, crooked nose – 'Waddya say? Huh, ya punks?' he growls through tiny, gritted teeth – 'Humphrey Bogart eh.'

Skud's blinded by the flashing suit, but he can't help but notice that for some strange reason his partner has forgotten the footwear, unless of course he simply prefers that flat, black plastic pair on his feet – 'Ye noa buy shoes?' he asks, almost, impertinently.

Barney doesn't bat an eyelid – 'Shoes? Ye aff yer fuckin heid? Ye kin steal shoes, ur jist get a pair aff some halfwit fur fucksake. S'he fuckin stupit?' he asks Jake.

Karen appears bearing three lagers and a smile. The last fifty is lying beside the other bank notes, by the till – 'Oh my. Widye look at him eh. James Cagney sittin there eh. That musta cost ye a fortune, eh? Where dae you dae yer shoppin?' she probes.

Barney smirks with pride – 'Aye, darlin. Three hunner quid fur the suit. Burtons' Mens Wear. Only the best. Eh, time dae ye finish then?' he asks, leering openly. The look, filled with perversion and sexual intent, is relentless – 'Might take ye fur a drink. Huv ye got yer ain hoos? Geez anurra three double whiskies while yer at it,' he indicates with three stubs on a hand, and another fifty – and that wink.

Karen hides her revulsion – 'Oh listen tae um, eh. Yer noa slow are ye. Oh, well, who knows. Al have tae close the bar and things. Ye never know wit might happen later, dae ye?' she calls, wiggling her hips all the way back to the bar.

Barney's face is bright red with sexual arousement. He nudges Jake – 'Fuckinhell eh! Didje see that there? She's burstin fur it. Aw here. Am nippin that the night. That's me goat ma hole. Bitin the fuckin leg aff ur, the big cow!' he slavers.

Jake knows that *he's* the one she fancies. Called him handsome, didn't she. Barney? Who does he think he's kidding? He throws back his long, jet-black hair. Birds? Can't resist him, he decides. The Levi's slouch further down into the worn, beer-sodden old velvet seating running along the back wall of the lounge – Barney, eh.

Jake's watching every movement in the bar, blurry as it may well be with the amount of alcohol swallowed in the past hour. He never sat with his back to a door. Never since that day he had seen that guy almost get big Clint Eastwood, in *The High Plains Drifter*. Imagine? Sitting in a barber's chair with your back to the door, and the barber with an open razor? He is about to concede that the man who had made his day had got the baddies first, when two characters appear in the main bar.

'Coppers,' he hisses. He could smell them a mile off – 'You kerryin, Skud? Thurs only two ey, thum.' Skud, too, had clocked them – 'S'that Untouchable mob. Fucksake,' he slurs, reaching up his sleeve for the blade – 'Ma fuckin burds leathur. Okay, Jake. Wi gaun ahead wi these two pricks? Right. Fuck thum. Av goat a steakie,' he confirms.

Barney had never been involved in violence, apart from the odd occasions when he'd happened to be on the receiving end of a blunt instrument, an iron bar maybe, or that common old household hammer – but this?

He's taking the horrors – 'Wit? Ur you's two aff yer fuckin heids? Noo jist calm doon. Thur jist talkin tae the barmaid. Blades? Aw, naw. Here they come. Jake. Don't. Al take the derry, okay. It's only a fraud fur fucksake, son. Don't dae anythin,' he pleads.

Both Jake and Skud lean forward in their chairs as the two coppers come over to their table. Confrontations with the police had been a part of their lives. An arrest meant a battering. That's just the way things were – had always been. Coppers, courts, jail, an extra set of stitches and a few broken batons – no big deal.

Barney? This was just another capture. You didn't pull blades on the coppers – these guys ran the show.

Blades? That was asking for serious trouble.

You bunged them – 'Eh, how ye's daen, lads? A pint?' he asks.

'Naw. How you daen then, Barney? New suit?' smirks the smaller detective.

Barney is on his feet – 'Aye. Eh noa bad. Ye sure? Ye's noa wanta drink?' he begs.

Tom's assessing who he's going to knock out first – Jake or Skud. He feels the hatred emanating from their pores. He judges both to be right-handed. One of them seems too drunk to reach whatever he's carrying, but those blue, hate-filled eyes might take his baton to put a wee glaze over them. He would definitely have to keep an eye on him. He positions himself to the right of Jake. This would leave little room for him to pull out a weapon. Yes, it's all under control. Jerry, too, was ready – 'Whit's happenin then, Barney?' he continues, pressing the issue, sniffing out the money

Barney shrugs his shoulders – 'Jist huvin a pint,' he replies.

Jerry grins – 'Where didye get the money?'

Barney perseveres – 'Bookie's.'

Tom's watching Jake. His Highland brain fathoming the next move. Oh dear. These daft laddies, eh. A good kick up the arse'd do them the world of good. A good kick up the arse—

WOOOFFFFFFFFFFFFFFFFFFFF!

Jake's knee'd Tom in the balls. He rams the nut on him and the crunching sound of his broken nose echoes in his ears like the wailing of a wounded bagpipe, as he begins to fall. That huge frame hits the floor, like a sack of potatoes.

Skud has the steak knife out, lunging towards Jerry – 'C'monnnn! Ya fuckin bam ye!' Jerry falls backward. Fuck! What's happened? In his desperation to dodge that steak knife hitting him on the jaw, his trousers drop around his ankles!

'KARENNNNNNNNN!' he's squeeling.

'KARENNNNNNNNN!' crashing over tables.

Karen's in state of shock as the two young men run through the bar swinging a blade at punters, and screaming – 'C'MONNNNNNNNNN! SHAMROCKKKKK!'

Barney hasn't moved. He's standing with his hands in the air. Nothing to do with me stamped all over him – 'Jesus Christ,' he mumbles.

Tony folds his paper, tucks it into a pocket, finishing his pint before leaving – 'Fuckin young team. Canny go anywer es days,' he mutters.

He does a double take at the door – 'Fuck me, man. Widye jist lookit that. Lookit they underpants. Right up es bum,' he sniggers – 'My God, eh.'

Jake and Skud have left their jackets behind in their escape – plus most of the money. Skud reassures his partner – 'Fuck it! We kin dae anurra turn!' he exclaims – 'We kin jump a counter ur sumthin.'

Jake isn't pleased. That was his best leather jacket back there. He knows the pub will be swarming with police by now – 'That big fuckin prick! That big fuckin bam! Here! That big cow musta phoned thum. Am gonny fuckin rip hur fuckin jaw wide open. Al bet ye she stuck us in. The stupit cow. Am gonny rip hur fuckin jaw,' he swears.

Skud agrees without question – 'Aye, the big fuckin boot. Did you gie ur a tip?'

Jake turns to him – 'Ye kiddin? Right. Much ye goat?' he asks.

Skud empties his pockets – 'Two hunner quid an some change,' he replies. The Untouchables will be looking for them all over Glasgow. They're not stupid. Jake decides to lie low until dark before making any moves – 'Right. C'mon. Get a taxi tae the Odeon. The *Cuckoo's Nest* is oan there. Wull stay there tae the pubs shut an then we kin dae that big cow when it's dark, right?' he states.

Skud, too, thinks this is the best idea – 'Aye Jake, right!' Big Clint doesn't get to make his day after all.

Jake's still trembling from the adrenalin rush – 'Stupit cunts, man. Didye see Barney? Hauns in the air? Oh, nuthin tae dae wi me, boss!' he mimics.

Jerry's terrified face flashes before his eyes – 'Didye get that cunt wi the blade? Here! Didye see that big yin? A put um right oot, the cunt!' he continues, laughing.

Skud knows that he missed, but it was a close shave for the detective – 'Am noa really sure. Fuckin shat it, the prick. Didye see es troosers?' he asks.

Jake's laughing hysterically – 'Aye! Wit happened there?

A knee'd that big yin right in the baws, but that urra yins troosers? Didye hear um? KARRRREEEENNNN!'

Skud, too, is infected by the hysteria – 'Aye! They jist fell doon! Paira fuckin bams, eh. C'monnnnnn! Fuckinnnnn Bammmmmms!' he screams at no one.

The Woodside is black with uniformed policemen. Tom's big Highland testicles have been escorted by ambulance to the Royal Infirmary. His nose is broken from the blow of the head-butt – a direct hit on the bridge.

Karen's shaking with shock – 'Oh my god! Oh my god! Poor Tom!'

Jerry is holding his trousers up with one hand while the other is gripped around a fat neck – 'Right, you cunt. They two bastards. Who ur they?' he's screeching through clenched teeth.

Barney, the old die hard, holds out. A baton smashes over his head, knocking him to the floor, unconscious, which is where he wants to be, at least until they get him to a police station – 'Ughhhh,' he feigns, hitting the deck.

Jerry's bursting blood vessels – 'Get this FUCKER doon the road! BASTARDS!'

Barney is thrown onto the floor of the van, but prefers the boots resting on his skull to a razor across his jaw for grassing. Jerry grabs the jackets, pocketing the bank notes, before the uniforms notice anything – 'Here. Take these fuckin rags. Search thum. A photograph, anythin. A want these two cunts the night!' he orders a rookie.

Barney remains unconscious during the journey, but he makes a miraculous recovery just as he's dragged to the police bar – 'Wer uma? Av been assaulted!' he claims.

Boab doesn't bat an eyelid – 'Aye eh. Might have known. Right then. Wit address are we residing at these days then, Bernard?' he asks.

The glare from the suit catches his attention – 'Who are we tonight then? No, don't tell me, Edward G. Robinson? Right, Bernard. Belt, an shoelaces.'

He turns to the turnkey – 'Many's in number three? Six? Jerry shift that wee coloured gentleman? That's fine. Okay, number three it is.'

Barney displays that legendary legal expertise – 'Here, haud oan. Av been assaulted. How did a get here?' he demands to know.

Boab continues writing – 'Cut to the head. Right, that's recorded. That'll be a police assault and resistin arrest now too. Happy now, Edward G? Is that a spot of blood on yer new suit? Dear, dear,' he grins.

Barney has his defence prepared now, he's more than happy – 'S'long as it states that ma heid's split open. Av never been charged wi assault in forty years. You know that yerself, Boa . . .' he almost completes.

Boab chews the eraser on top of his pencil – 'Put um in three,' he scribbles.

Johnny's laughing when he sees who comes bundling into the cell – 'Here! Watch it, son. Suit's Burtons Mens Wear,' yelps Barney – 'Johnnny! Fuck me. How ye daen? Oh, Jesus Christ,' he whispers out of the side of his face – 'Jake an Skud. Think thur in bother. Battered two ey the Untouchables. Took nearly a grand aff me. The cu . . . Eh. Wit ye laffin at?' he asks.

Johnny doesn't say much – 'Ach, Auld Barney eh. When ye gonny chuck it? Yer past it, auld yin,' he smiles knowingly.

Barney becomes indignant — 'Past it? Humphh. The hell wid you know? Av been oot graftin fore you wur born, McGinty,' he declares with a twirl — 'Check the suit. Look at that thing you're wearin. A green suit? Paddy's market? Fuckin cheek! Look at ye. Ye look a ginger boattle. A fuckin boattla limeade.'

Johnny folds his arms, leans against the steel wall, head cocked to one side, eyes up the flashing silver zoot suit — 'Ur ye kiddin? Listen, auld yin. The Paki's been dun tae. That fat poof took um away tae make a statement. Guy's shitin umself,' he says. He's waited a long time for this — 'By the way. The muneys aw forgeries. Guy's a first offender tae. Think the boay's bumped ye, eh. Magine that. A first offender as well.' He draws blood — 'Aye. Yer past it.'

Barney blanches indignantly. Barney, conned? A first offender? — 'WIT? DUDS? Aye, right. Nae danjur! You're at it, ya cunt ye. Wull were is ey then?' he demands as proof.

Johnny doesn't move — 'Told ye. Fatso took um away. Wants a statement. Aboot this wee fat guy, called Barney,' he grins.

The audience of the cell are all ears as the mystery unfolds. All eyes are now looking at the blinding flash of material as it hits the cell door's tiny window — 'SHABBYYYYY! SHABBYYYYYYYY! YA BLACK BASTARD! YOU BETTER NO GRASS!' it roars.

Barney's face is flushed with rage. Con him? The dirty black bastards. Imagine doing a a stunt like that? Right out of order. Dud money! Imagine it? What a showing up. Wait until those two other headcases find oot. Jake'll rip the faces off these two black cunts. Check this cunt as well, he thinks. Johnny dangerous. Be standing on one leg next. Hard men, eh.

Limping about on one leg. Do they think they're flamingos? Eh? Look at him. Done up like a bird. Look at the hair? Poof. Definitely, he concludes.

Johnny and the cell occupants are observing the frown – 'So, Barney. Wit ye gonny dae aboot it?' he asks.

Barney knows he's being noised up, but – 'Durty fuckin informers! That's wit they ur! They wid cut thur fuckin baws aff if it wis the army. That's wit wid happen. Aye!' he puffs proudly – 'Sojurs didny tolerate any informers in thur ain camps,' declares that voice of the unconscientious objector – 'Jake'll chib they two! You wait an see!' The unknown sojur speaketh. Barney, World War Two non-contender, has declared World War Three. The pacifist with the simple philosophy of 'no chance', has finally been awoken, and is now thirsty for blood, preferably black blood – 'Jist aswell am non-vialent!'

The battlefield of his mind is a river of scarlet, but the mood has turned black. He just can't believe that he has been delivered the sucker blow – by a daft Paki at that. The entity of the non is enraged, he has been humiliated. He, however, he of the non-this, and the non-that, he is not cannon fodder. No, he is an earner, an organiser, one who instructs, a general no less.

He dispatches through the hole – the decision, the declaration, that message of war – 'SHABBY! JAKE'LL BE LOOKIN FUR YE! AYE! WI A FUCKIN BAYONIT'

Chapter Four

MEANWHILE, JAKE IS in the dimension he lives his life through. The blue ice melting in the corners of his eyes is forming tears – 'Bastards,' he mutters through a mouthful of crisps – 'A fuckin liberty.'

Jack Nicholson, having just been lobotomised, is now being smothered to death by a believer in euthanasia; a compassionate fellow patient. At that very point in the film, a wave passes through another brain, in the audience of *One Flew Over the Cuckoo's Nest* – 'That's the way am gaun oot,' decides that brain.

Skud, too, is mesmerised by the haunting music floating through those vacated spaces between his ears. Pink Floyd had been tenants there since his first trip. *Dark Side of The Moon*, *Us and Them*, *Meadows*, *Umagumma* – but this flute? – 'Bastards, Jake, eh,' he nudges, knowing that his pal would do the same for him if he was cabbaged up. If? Vegetation was more a question of time than possibility. Skud was halfway there already. There was not much left to vegetate in that vast reservoir of emptiness – 'Big Indian's bran new, eh. An at music, man. Fuckin brulliant,' he says.

Jake's simple, but acknowledged, 'Shut it,' hides the tears of those cold eyes.

So deeply moved are they by the film, they can barely talk – 'S'that the end?'

Jake rises – 'Aye. C'mon. That's it.'

The darkness of night embraces the two figures as they make

their way back towards Maryhill Road, and the Woodside Inn – 'Time is it, Skud?'

Skud looks up at the sky – 'Must be aboot ten,' he replies.

Jake feels the drop in the temperature bite into his bones after the comforting warmth of the film house – 'Widdye think? Brulliant film winnit. That Ratchet bastard wis oan es back aw the time. See? Fuckin wumin. Cunts, the lottey thum,' he comments.

Skud agrees – 'Aye, man. Big Indian wis brilliant, wint ey? See when ey spoke? Fuck, a wis like that!' he exclaims, stunned – 'Aye! A thought ey wis really deef an dumb so a did. Fuckin shows ye, dinnit. Sum actur, eh.'

Jake's never been fooled though – 'Nah. A knew at the beginnin. Some size, wint ey? That bit wi the sink. Right throo the windae tae. That musta took some strength. Ye got that blade there? Right, geez it,' he commands.

Skud hands him the steak knife – 'Ye want me tae chib ur?' he asks.

Jake slips the blade into a rolled-up newspaper – 'Na. You keep a taxi runnin roon the corner. Jist say yer waitin fur some cunt, okay. Naw, al dae this cow maself,' he says.

He feels the knife's handle as they swagger up Woodside Road – 'Barney won't grass. Tell ye that. Never grassed any cunt. Right. Noo you goan get a taxi an geez a shout right away. An mind. Get the cunt tae keep the engine runnin, okay Skud,' he orders.

Skud steps out onto the road to watch for a taxi – 'Nae borra. Al whistle, okay?'

Jake's waiting outside the pub for what seems an eternity, but after just a few minutes hears that familiar whistle piercing the night. Skud reappears within seconds of their signal –

'Right, av got a taxi roon the corner. Sure ye don't want me tae dae it? Okay then. Driver thinks am waitin fur ma burd,' he says, slapping his partner on the back.

Jake pulls the blade from the newspaper – 'Right, beat it.'

He waits a few seconds before moving. Skud will be in the taxi . . . now. The punters in the bar, mostly half-bevvied, don't notice the figure striding through the front door – or the steak knife by his side. They're too busy swallowing or shouting. Some may even be having sly glances at the big blonde's arse as she's putting money in the till – 'Aye, two lagers cummin up in a minu—' she's calling, unaware of the savagery coming at her from behind.

Jake jumps the counter and before she's completed the sentence, banged her twice over the head, and whacked her across the face from behind with the blade.

Thunk! Thunk! Thunk!

He's back over the counter and heading through the door before anyone realises what has happened. He listens to the scream before leaving. Then rounds the corner, and slides into the taxi – 'The Maryland, driver,' he says calmly.

Skud's looking at him – 'S'Dawn there?' he asks pointedly.

Jake's grin confirms he's done the business – 'Aye. Said she'll meet us later,' he says, passing back the blade – 'Here,' he whispers – 'S'covered in blud. Three rapid. Think she'll be needin the paroxide tae fix that hair.'

Skud laughs loudly – 'Fuckin brulliant! Hurry up driver. Canny get in efter eleven. A think al get a bitta blaw, huv a party later, eh? On ye fuckin go, man. Auld Barney eh? His heid'll be burstin as well!' he shouts.

The taxi driver knows the score, he doesn't even look in the rear-view mirror to check the faces. Pure trouble. You can smell it. He just wants to get home tonight – in one condition – with his face intact, and free of black thread. Animals, the lot of them, he thinks to himself. They're on something, or more likely done something. Not his business. No hospitals for him, he decides, wisely.

The Royal Infirmary is having a busy night with the casualty rates, particularly from a pub in Woodside Road. The Central Police Station too, are having their problems in the casualty department. Karen and Tom are but a ward away from each other – only her ward is purely for patients needing emergency surgery. Whereas those big Highlander balls are merely under observation, with a view to compensation, and a possibility of that wee deputy inspector's post in Edinburgh. However, far more serious matters are about to unfold back at the police station, a sequence of events of the unnatural kind, the inexplicable explainable police kind.

Jerry, the detective, wants to interview Barney – 'Take him tae the interview room, an then al see the Paki,' he tells the female turnkey. He watches her walk away. A nice arse that wee thing. He looks up. Here's this scum. Fucking scummmm. Barney's very presence fills Jerry with rage as he sits down on the chair before him, a slight smile on his square face – 'Right, Boone. Names. A want names. Your right in trouble, son,' he snarls.

Son? Barney had been serving four years' hard labour when this *boy* had been in his nappies – 'Trouble? Don't think so,' he says with a sigh.

Jerry bangs his fist on the table as he leaps from his chair. His sweaty face is an inch from his captive – 'Don't you fuckin get wide wi me, son. The rest ey the money?' he screams – WHACKKKKKKKKKK! – 'An fuckin names!'

Barney is built to absorb such blows. Son? Should never have said that. Most other coppers were more amiable. He touches the nick over his eyebrow. He'll have huge black eyes, just in time for his court appearance in the morning – 'D'ye hit me there? *Son?*' he asks, smirking.

Jerry's brain disfunctions with that legendary temper of his – 'WHITTT? YOU FUCKIN LITTLE BASTARD!'

WHACKKKKKKKKKK!

WHACKKKKKKKKKK!

When Barney regains consciousness, he smiles – 'Sixty convictions. Nain fur violent affences, ever. When Auld Santa sees this face, *you're* in trouble, eh, *son*. Noo get me ma legal aid form. Am an auld age pensioner, by the way. Ye always batter auld age pensioners? Son?'

Barney's smiling, grotesquely. His swollen mouth and eyes creasing into patches of disfigured flesh – 'Ad like to see the desk sergeant noo. Makin an afficial complaint, against you, *son*. Ohh, Goddd. Am gettin pains inside ma heid. A docturrr, a need a do . . .' he sneers, feigning it all the way to the floor.

Jerry is losing it – completely. He runs, ramming his captive through doors, throwing the elderly street urchin down three flights of stairs to the holding cells – 'MOVE! YA FUCKER YE!'

The female turnkey is well acquainted with drunks. The sight of blood is just part of a weekend night shift duty. The detective's dishevelled appearance, however, gives her cause for concern – 'You alright, sir?' she asks.

Hate-filled eyes swirl upon her – 'Gimme they fuckin keys you!' they spit – 'Get him in wi the rest ey they fuckin animals! Lumpa FUCKIN shite. MOVE YA BASTARD!'

Together they throw the dead weight back into number three – 'BOSS! BOSS! FUCK! GEZZ SOME WATER! BASTARDS!'

CLANG.

Jerry's pouring with sweat from his exertions – 'Geez they keys! Number's that black bastard in? He knows somethin! Thur aw innit, the bastards. The whole fuckin lot ey thum. Bastards. Big Tom. Ma fuckin mate. Al kill this cunt,' he slavers.

The young policewoman pulls nervously at the bunch of keys – 'Oh c'mon. Goodness sakes!' she mumbles reassuringly – 'There. The rubber mat cell,' she says, handing him the keys – 'He's been awfy quiet. There. You can jist hand them in to Boab. Am finished in half an hour anyway so—'

He snatches the keys from her – 'Aye, right, c'mon, c'mon, right, right, cheerio.'

My, my. The manners of it. Drunks, fights and blood. They were one thing. She had steeled herself in the face of brutality. This was, after all, male territory. She had to live with abuse on a daily basis. Why else would they have her doing late shifts in the holding cells? Job experience? The company? The nineteen-year-old was no fool. She knew what to expect, but this?

She marches off without another word. The cheek of it, she thinks, climbing the flight of stairs. A detective sergeant, too? Well, to hell with him, she decides, heading for a nice hot tea in the canteen. *Starsky and Hutch* on the night? she wonders, leaving the detective to get on with it. Wouldn't like to be in that poor Pakistani man's shoes.

* * *

Johnny must have taken cramp. He's switched walls, but leaning, the exclusion zone still in force against those watery eyes around him – 'Take it ye didny dae a statement en Barney?' he asks the heap on the floor.

Barney rolls over onto his back – 'Jeez,' he says, sitting up – 'Ooofff. Took a few sore yins there wi that bastard, but eh,' he groans.

He climbs to his feet – 'Am walkin the morra. You wait n see. Fuck me. A banged ma elbow er but a wound that cunt right up. Aye. Am walkin, McGinty. You wait n see,' he smiles, slyly.

The face looks like a purple balloon. Three-hundred quid's worth of silver material is in ruins – 'Aw, wid ye look it ma suit!' he exclaims – 'Three-hunner fuckin quid! Right doon the fuckin drain! Look at it, man! Ach, it's noa like the auld days. Aye, maybe it is time tae chuck it, but am walkin the morra. Jist you wait n see,' he grins, brushing down his red-stained silver suit.

Johnny bristles as the older man splats the caked, reddish-green contents of his nose in the direction of the urinal – 'Watch the fuckin gear, Barney. Am warnin ye,' he says quietly, but firmly – 'So did ye make a statement?' he continues.

Barney isn't listening to the questions, it would seem. He's frowning, looking down at the floor, the concrete floor, the cold concrete floor, with its rough texture – 'Aw, here. Ma shoes! Thuv took ma fuckin shoes, an ma soaks! That's every time am dun. Wit's this place cummin tae eh?'

He pretends to head-butt the cell door – 'Blamin me tae fur that bank robbery the urra day. A mean, ME-EE?' he pleads – BANG! BANG! BANG! – 'ME-EEEE? EHHH?'

The performance comes off. A bank? Jaws slacken below

those watery eyes. They are *enthralled* – 'Robbin banks! Me-eeee? At ma age, fur fucksake? A don't know, eh. Honest, it's noa like the auld days. Sixty-seven years of age tae, eh?'

Johnny's grin is irritating him, but he perseveres – 'This is aw that black bastard's fault, ye know,' he declares, assessing the potential footwear – 'Pakis! Ye jist canny trust these people kin ye? A mean. Take unemployment fur example. A mean. We'd aw have joabs if it wisny fur these people. A mean, jist fur a start. Wid we aw be sittin in this fuckin pitch? Eh?' he asks.

The black holes gape – 'NAWW! Coz we'd aw huv FUCKIN JOABS!'

The lion rampant, ramps, and rages – 'Aye eh! A decent fuckin livin! That's aw that a want. Treatin US like animuls tae! S'they Pakis! Am tellin ye! S'they cunts! It's US! US! That ur Scottish! Achhhhh! Wit's the point, eh, men?'

The legal expert has taken the floor – 'Auld Santa oan the morra? Jeez. Ey hates the sight ey me tae. Oh well, that's the bail fucked. They coppers'll be laughin at me tae. Means av goat tae go up tae court in ma bare feet noo. Lookin like a fuckin Apache.' He laughs – 'Aye eh. Ja-fuckin-ronimo.'

Two teenage, half-innocent eyes have taken an interest – 'Wit ye dun fur, mistur?' they ask, almost begging to lose their shoes.

Barney frowns for a moment, then, looking at the lad, he asks – 'Wit age ur you, son?'

Johnny spits in the urinal, watching the elasticity of his saliva as it drips to the floor almost like silk twine – 'Like a spider's web that stuff, eh,' he smirks.

The cycle of desperation evolves; dehydrated grey matter ignites, the provider of hope is about to provideth. This man who walks on concrete, feels no cold. For he hath walked this land before – he *knoweth* the unknown terrain.

The faithful followers of misfortune are about to follow. Their bare-footed elder has the powers of prophecy. The human gene of intelligence speaketh in tongues – 'Aye, Pakis. Cannyfuckintrustthum. Theblackbastards. Fuckininformers,' it sayeth.

Saab, though, is beyond providing information – of any kind. The detective kicking the door open is met with silence – 'RIGHT HECTOR! IT'S ME AGAIN! HERE CUNT!'

Sleeping? Where does this black bastard think he is? This cunt needs a few lessons! The detective, however, can no longer do any harm, can no longer terrorise what is no longer there.

He is surprised when the body doesn't budge, even after another kick – WHOOFFFFF! – 'MOVE, YA FUCKER! WIT THE FUCK! OH NO! JESUS! E'S DEID!' he gasps.

He grabs for his belt, but it's gone, gone with the soul of the dead man. – 'Fuck!' he hisses – 'Fuckkk!'

It's dug into the neck of the body. Tugging it loose he feels nothing for the dead man – only panic. Self-preservation insulates him from anything else. The eyes looking through him are just a Pakis.

His career's more important – *surely*.

Oh fuck! Tom. What does he do here? Oh, Jesus. McGinty! He did it! Blame him. That's it! McGinty! Oh fuck, Boone! A PF's release! That's it! Say the procurator fiscal's releasing him. Give him the cash. Say there's no evidence. He won't grass. He's from the auld mob. Yes. Calm down. Get the belt back. That's it. Calm down, man. Pull yourself together. That's it. Thaat's it. Easyyyy. Think this through. Thaaaat's it.

He pulls himself together, buckling his belt back on – 'Right noo, that's it,' he mutters to himself, leaving the death cell – 'Aye, that's it.'

A thought strikes like a thunderbolt – *SUICIDE!*

Suicide! That's it. C'mon, Jerry boy. That's more like it. Yes. A suicide. Get Barney away. Shut him up. It never happened. McGinty gave him a tanking. Moved the poor guy for his own safety. That's it. For his own safety. Fuck. It's just a Pakistani.

Barney can't believe his luck when the cell door opens – 'Right, Barney. Yer luck's in the night. Nae evidence. C'mon, move it. PF's release,' the detective orders.

Johnny lifts his head, but doesn't move – 'See ye – *grassssss.*'

CLANG – *Sssssssssssssssssssssssssssssss.*

The prophet grinneth – 'Fuck you.'

Barney sees feet as he passes the rubber-mat cell. They're black – 'Size a shoe dis he take, boss?' he asks.

The detective panics, for a moment – Fuck! The door!

He pulls it shut quickly – 'C'mon. Nevermind that yin. Here, stick that it yer tail. Right noo. Nae hard feelins, okay. An don't spend aw that in the wan shop. Oh, and, by the way, yer barred fae the Woodside,' he grins broadly, passing the forgeries – 'Tell they other two the same. Wull settle that another day. So jist keep yer mooth shut, okay?'

Barney didn't need to be told twice – 'Aye, boss. Suits me,' he replies, examining the bank notes – 'They duds right enough?'

Jerry just smiles – 'Duds? Don't know wit ye talkin aboot, auld yin.'

Boab, the desk sergeant, doesn't bother to look up – 'PF's

release. Happened tae yer face, Bernard?' he asks, pencil in mid air – waiting.

Barney knows the score – 'Ma face? Nuthin wrang wi ma face. S'wrang wi yours eh? S'wrang wi yours eh, get it?' But no one's laughing.

Boab's pencil is still in mid air – 'Any complaints? No? Fine. Okay, Barney. Stay oot ey trouble. Oh, an a wid see an optician aboot that suit,' he says, scribbling. Was that a smile?

Jerry laughs at the figure barefooting it through the doors – 'Auld Barney eh. An auld character, eh. Noa like that anamul doon the stairs, that McGinty.'

Boab finally looks up – 'S'there a problem?' he asks. The twinkling blue eyes have seen it all – heard it all – twice, and more.

When Jerry finishes with the suicide report, that bored old pencil is replaced with the little, rarely used, red eraser at the opposite end of the leaded stick – 'Aye. Need tae watch that temper ey yours, son. Ach. A wee enquiry, an it's all over. A belt? Don't see any belt doon here,' he says, tapping the property card – 'Musta hid it under the kaftan. These personal property cards never lie.'

He pulls out the property bag – 'Here, leave that in the cell,' he says, pulling out the dead man's leather belt – 'Ye finished duty efter the arrest, okay?'

Jerry nods – 'Thanks, Boab. Al find oot who these other two wur. Boone won't tell us enathin. Scared incase they chib um probably. Big Tam's nose wis broke. These two bampots came fae the back. We wurny expectin it. Right oot the blue, blades. Right then. Al go an see the big man in the mornin. Bastards, al catch they two, Boab. Pity aboot that Paki. Al write ma report the night.'

Boab blows the card clean – 'Aye. Pakis, eh. Say it's gonny be swelterin the morra again. Might last a few mer days. So thur sayin. Takin the missus tae Cyprus. Right. Leave this yin doon the stairs wi me. Gie Tom ma regards,' he says, the wee excited eraser getting to rewrite the history of yet another statistic, one more fatality – 'Oh, by the way. Thur wis another incident up at the Woodside. Ach. Leave it tae the morra. Probably be too bizzy the night. Be drunks ur sumthin. S'this heat, eh. Night then. Al see ye in the mornin. Al sort this business. That McGinty might dae.'

Jerry pushes through the doors, into the darkness – 'Right. Night, Boab.' Black bastard, he thinks. Hardly fucking touched him. Now there's this fucking stupid report to fill in for the morning. Black bastard. Who the fuck cares? Some daft Paki? Committing suicide? Fuck them all. They should never have been allowed to stay in the country in the first place. That could have been the promotion up in the air. All because of a fucking Paki – 'Sammy fuckin Davis.'

He laughs to himself – 'Auld Barney eh. Tough auld bastard. S'he daen involved wi these black bastards?'

Sanji listens to his brother – 'Cops?' he asks incredulously – 'How? Did the cops get Saab? Are you sure, Ra? How would they know about the money?' he repeats – 'Wi better shut the shop. But how could the cops know anything? Maybe Saab left, for a juice or cigarettes or something?'

Rashid is certain – 'Naw, Sanji, they knew. They wur lookin inside thur van. Saab's in jail, he's been lifted, am tellin ye, Sanji.'

Sanji shakes his head – 'But Ra, how would they know? It disnae make any sense, so calm down. Saab might be okay, and anyway he would never tell them about us, not his brothers.'

'Aye? But what if?' counters the younger brother – 'Wit dae a say? N'wit if the cops lift me? Wit am a supposed tae say?' he cries – 'A knew this would be trouble . . .'

Sanji interrupts – 'Oh, I see, it's all my fault?' he asks accusingly – 'S'alright when cash comes in, but my fault if something goes wrong? You two were just to hand over that money and come back with anoraks. Now there's this? Cops?'

Rashid shrugs – 'S'your idea n the furst place,' he mumbles.

'What?' snaps Sanji – 'I see, first bit of pressure and it's all my fault,' he repeats – 'Next time . . . Oh, God.'

Rashid turns to find his elderly mother standing in the doorway to the small kitchen.

'I hear trouble!' she states – 'Why fighting in this house?'

'We were just talking, Mother. Rashid and I just talking. Go back upstairs, please. What? I said we were just t-a-l-k-i-n-g!' gesticulates the elder brother – 'Go back upstairs, and let us talk together.'

The old woman allows her son to guide her back up the stairs – 'Watch the television, Sanji make you nice tea. No, Mother, there is no fighting. Rashid and Sanji are good brothers. No, there is no fighting in this house, Mother.'

Rashid's feeling more anxious – 'Wit happens if the cops come here? You'll have tae talk tae thum,' he says – 'F'they see me am dun.'

Sanji takes him by the elbow – 'Look, stop panicking,' he soothes – 'If they come here I will handle things. We've done nothing wrong. Think about it, Ra. The van's nothing to do with us, you're just in a panic.'

Rashid looks forlornly through the windows to their back garden – 'Al hide,' he states, matter-of-factly.

'Sure, Ra, leave this to me,' his brother assures him – 'We'll just wait first to see what happens, then I'll know what to do. So just calm down and stay in and I'll close the shop for the rest of the day, okay?'

Rashid nods in agreement – 'Okay, but . . .'

Sanji guides his brother upstairs – 'We'll just sit it out, nothing'll happen I bet. Saab's probably on his way home. Anyway, panic won't get us anywhere so, just wait and we'll see what happens.'

Saab, he thinks. Why can't he do anything right? All he had to do was hand over that fake money and walk away. How could he be in jail? he asks himself again. The men were crooked businessmen, he'd said to him – 'Nae problum.'

Glasgow fly men, he laughs. That's what his brothers think they are, two fly men. His Mother could barely string a sentence together in English, let alone Glaswegian. He'd had to look after everything, the family business, and also Saab and Rashid.

'I should send them home, see how they like it there,' he mutters to himself – 'Yes, let them see how people lived back there in Pakistan.'

Chapter Five

BARNEY FLITS DOWN through the lanes barefoot, until eventually he comes upon the taxi rank at Charing Cross – 'Yoker, driver. Twinty-three Boclair Street. S'oan the left haun side as ye go in. Wooof. Stull gets cauld at night, eh?' he remarks.

The driver swings the cab around – 'Aye. Say it'll be roastin the morra again. S'even warmur than the contanint. Hunner degrees yisterday. S'always the same, innit? Rain wan minut an scorchin the next,' he replies.

Barney brushes grit from the soles of his feet – 'Aye. Wee maw ey mines. Took a turn s'mornin. Aye. Jist gaun up tae see she's awright. Noa used tae this heat. Oh, ye jist canny tell thum kin ye? Sittin oot in the back aw day. An then they canny understaun how they get sunstroke? Know wit a mean, son?' he sniggers.

The driver looks at the face in the mirror – 'Aye. Wur maws, eh?' he agrees.

Barney looks out of the window. A few days at his mother's house. Get fed, and rest up a bit. Time to distance himself from those other two, he thought. All that nonsense and for what? Forgeries? It had been embarrassing to think that he had been caught at his own game. That was bad enough. Then that carry on with the police too? Jake did have potential but he really was off his head. Violence? What had that to do with earning a few quid? He did like the boy. He was just far too dangerous. He had that feeling about him. A murder waiting to happen, he thought.

The driver calls over the noise of the meter – 'Twinty-three, didye say?'

Barney looks up – 'Aye. Twinty-three, son.'

No, it was time to move on. Violence had the hallmarks of a mug. Someone without brains. The image of that detective's trousers falling down flashed through his mind. Jesus. What a sight. Why had they let him out? McGinty had said that the Pakistani had grassed them all. Nothing added up. Was there something he was missing?

He felt the bundle in his trouser pocket. A copper giving him the forgeries back? Had that been to shut him up? They had taken truncheons to him before in the past. They didn't just throw you out. Definitely not to hide a couple of black eyes. No, there had to be another explanation.

He needed time to think. A few days to reorganise his thoughts – 'S'that us there noo, son?' he called, looking out the window – 'Must be in ur bed. The room lights ur oan anyway.'

He reaches into his jacket pocket – 'Much didye say, son? Och. Wid ye believe it. Av left ma wallet in that bloody hotel. Achh. Listen take ma jaikit the noo, son. Al jist nip up an get the fare. Four quid? Call it a fiver,' he winks – 'Noa be five minutes.'

The driver looks at his watch – 'Nae bother,' he sighs. He watches Barney disappear up the front close. There was always one, he thought. The drunks were the worst though. Vomiting all over the seats Then refusing to pay their fare. He looked at the meter for a moment. The old guy had seemed alright – but. He left it running. A fare was a fare. He had to earn a living – keeps the wolves away from the door he thinks, fidgeting and drumming his fingers on the steering wheel – 'S'keepin um anyhow?' he grumbled.

Barney was still trying to vault the railings of the back court – 'Oof. Christsakes. Too fuckin auld fur this lark,' he mutters. He makes another attempt to swing his leg up, makes it and hangs – 'S'better. Oooya cunt ye.' He balances himself before pushing forward – 'Right. GO-OHYA!'

BRRRRRRRRRRRRRRRRRRRRRR-IP!

The sound of a paper bag bursting erupts in the night. That draught blowing straight up between his cheeks can mean only one thing – 'Christ. Ma strides!'

He completes the vault to find his shirt tail exposed through the seam – 'Fur Godsake! Better no let enybody see me,' he moans, drawing the tail up into his bum, as he runs across the back court to his mother's real address.

Auld Bessie had been darning socks by the fireside for most of the night. She had just been about to go bed when she heard the knock at the front door – 'That'll be oor Bernard,' she sighed.

She lights the gas ring on the cooker as she passes the scullery – 'Be starvin. Wantin tea. Aye. Am cummin, son,' she shouts.

Barney brushes past her – 'M'noa here maw, case the door goes.'

Bessie shuffles back to the kitchen and starts to stir the soup – 'Yer noa in, didye say, son?' she calls through – 'Aye eh. Yer an awful boy.'

Barney peeps through the curtains – 'Taxi drivers. Shood be in thur beds, the cunts.'

Bessie had been through it all before; the police, the courts, the prison visits, but he was her only son, born out of wedlock. He'd had little chance in life. When his father had fled before the birth, she'd been left to face the shame of pregnancy, and all the horror of teenage parenthood – there had been no room at the inn for her when she emerged from Rotten Row Maternity Hospital in 1909.

Bessie's Catholic parents had been deeply shamed by their daughter. How could their own sixteen-year-old daughter have done this to them? She had barely left school. In the face of everything they had done to bring her up properly, sexual intercourse with a man had destroyed their hopes for her future. Leaving only a bastard boy behind as a token of her promiscuity.

What would the priest think of them? And the neighbours? These had been the pressing questions of the times.

The beatings her father had given her on discovering the pregnancy should have been enough to make Bessie see reason, but no. Her refusal to have the bastard baby adopted had been unthinkable. She herself had made it impossible. She alone would have to bear that burden – for the rest of her life.

Barney had never encountered another man in their household. His mother was still a virgin, like all mothers.

'Hungry, son? Plate a pea soup dae? Goan ben tae the fire. Soup'll noa be a minute. Be gled tae be hame again, eh?' she asked.

Barney had no memory of home outside this house but his mother had had to wait six years on the corporation housing list before being housed. She had been living in her house for sixty-one years. Building a home for them hadn't been easy, but she had no complaints. She loved her house, with its two bedrooms, and inside toilet. The chair by the fireside had been her companion of twenty years. Many's the night she'd sat in the darkness, wrapped in her woollen shawl, staring into the fire with just the wireless playing in the background. Every creaking floorboard, every leaking tap – the soul of the building – had been imbued in her heart. The house had all the memories she had ever wanted to remember.

Her father she had heard, had died before the war. A bottle of whisky a day had killed him. Her mother had died some years later, but their daughter hadn't been allowed to attended either of the funerals. She hadn't met them since that day in 1909. They had both died having never set eyes on their grandson.

She had kept all his things from his childhood in amongst all the old coats she used for the beds during winter. His comics stacked high beside the little tin soldiers. Christmas annuals filled the shelves of almost every cupboard in the house. Their hardback covers had sometimes had to fill a hole in his shoes, but this had been the fabric of his memory, stored in there forever.

Now, as he stood before her, she remembered his impossible hair, that twinkle in his eyes, and cheeky smile – a wee rascal he'd been as a boy. She put down the soup beside him – 'Mer bread, son? S'thur enough salt in that? Oh lookit that. Bernard, did ye walk aw the way up here wi nae shoes oan, son? My God. Ye'll never learn. Wit's happened tae yer shoes?' she asked.

Barney supped the soup – 'Soup's great, hen. Aye. A ganga boys took ma shoes affey me. Any mer breed? Am starvin so am ur. Walked it.' He listens for a moment – 'Eh. S'that a taxi oot there?' he asks.

Bessie brought more bread – 'Wit's that, son? Gaun deaf. Needin tae get a hearin aid. A jist canny get up tae that doctur's. A taxi did ye say?' she asks.

Barney folds a slice and stuffs it into his mouth – 'S'noa shmmmnnna the shmmnnna same shmmmnnna umna is it?' he splutters.

Bessie smiled. What an awful boy. How many times had she told him not to speak with his mouth full – 'Eh son?'

Barney looks up from the plate, cleaning his teeth with his tongue – 'Slrrrup. Aherm. SNOATHESAMEISIT?' he roars through an avalanche of breadcrumbs.

Bessie nodded – 'Naw, s'noa, is it. Say ye wanted a taxi? Ye noa stayin here the night then? Av got yer bed ready tae? Al jist get tae mine then. Mer soup there if ye want. Mind put the lights off then, son. Nightyho. Aye eh.'

Barney rolls his eyes – 'Night, maw. See ye in the moarnin. Nightyho, eh.' He pulls the shawl up around his shoulders, settling into the chair for the night. He'd slept there a million times throughout his life. The chair was comfortable, soft, and a reassurance.

The fire flickered in the dark as he stared into eternity. He pulled the shawl up closer around his head. He'd feared shadows as a boy. The shawl guarded him from all the peripheral bogeymen waiting to catch him whenever he looked. He peeked out from behind his sanctuary just to make sure – old habits died hard.

The living room hadn't changed in years. The furniture was old as the hills. Even the wallpaper hadn't changed ever since he could remember, and yet everything was so well preserved. His mother had spent her whole life polishing furniture, and cleaning the house. Every night she had read parables from her black Bible. She had kept it by the fire all these years – 'S'summer an she's burning fires. Yer maw eh,' he chuckles. He touches the leather-bound cover, remembering many of the wonderful stories they had shared together. Her singing him to sleep. He had no memory of anger – only her sighs of resignation when there had been hard times – 'Aw, God luv ye, son.'

How he had longed to give her something, even a holiday, something better than this. She had been a good mother to him, and deserved something back from life, but that, like everything else, had a price.

He poked up a shower of sparks with the poker. The fire glowed fiercely for a moment and shrank again into cooling embers – 'Aye, yer wee maw, eh,' he sighed.

He held up one of the forged banknotes. They were all first-class forgeries. There was no doubt about that. He had nine-hundred quid's worth in twenty-pound notes. What to do with them. That was the question. He could make a good percentage by selling them at a cut rate. That was too simple. They were excellent work. Hadn't he fallen for them? He considered passing them himself in shops, but that would involve work. No, that wasn't for him, he had to profit from them, but without effort on his part. That was the name of the game after all – money for nothing.

He poked the fire again, scratching his chin. He watched tiny sparks explode. The pea soup had filled him, but hunger of another kind was keeping him awake. Nine-hundred quid. What to do with it. Where to play it out. How to do it successfully. How to turn the fake into the real. He fingered the worn leather of his mother's Bible. Where else but the good book for inspiration? He likened himself to that other prophet – 'Hhmm. The water intae wine, eh,' he muttered.

He stared into the fire. The fine particles of carbon hung suspended in the lum, like a human lung. Smoke, he thought. Why did people pollute themselves with that stuff? Paying for a poison that kills them? Then describing it as pleasure?

He frowned for a moment. Pleasure? The springboard for pleasure was desire and he knew only too well where that could lead. Quite suddenly, the purity of mathematics crystallised like a diamond in his brain – desire=pleasure=opportunity. The frown deepened. How to convert these three basic principles into the philosophy of life – commodity=exchange=profit.

He smiled. Greed – the greatest flaw in human nature. Behind that face hung a lolling tongue, desperate for more. His processes of deduction and market research clicked into auto-pilot – who had burgled what, and what were their prices?

Abracadabra – Chic Brogan!

Brogan. The name registered a positive connection to a recent spate of burglaries on privately owned newsagent shops. Brogan had been behind them; down through the ceiling, and avoid the floor. Avoiding the alarms limited the choice of goods, but that meant the sweeties alone were safe. Cigarettes and tobacco were kept on shelves to attract the attention of customers. No respectable burglar broke into a shop to simply steal sweeties.

Brogan. Yes – *modus operandi* – hole in the roof, speciality – tobacco.

He poked the fire. He was getting somewhere. Snout could be bought cheaply on the pavement, and re-sold again legitimately at a profit. He had good contacts who would fence cigarettes and tobacco.

Brogan would be easy to find – he liked young boys – 'Aye. Wee Brogan. He'll dae. A poof anyway, the wee cunt. Nae wunder nae cunt want's tae know um.'

Charles 'Chic' Brogan; criminal status – small-time poof.

The fire was going out. He pulled the shawl around his head. It was good to be home, he thought. He watched the embers shrink into warm char, listening to the crunching sound as tiny lumps fell into the grate. Only the house could be heard as he began to fall asleep. She creaked and groaned until silence overwhelmed the dream schedule of her two occupants. Nothing stirred in the night other than the wind. An occasional breeze signalled the presence of human beings.

BRRRRRRRRRRRRRRRRRRRR-P – 'Pardon me,' whispered a voice.

Barney had never farted in daylight without having to have his confession heard by a priest – 'God Bless me Father for I have Sinned.' He farted only at night – 'T'was not me. T'was the Wind.' No, he didn't fart in public, certainly not in the presence of his mother anyway.

Most 'good' Catholics developed a technique to avoid detection in the event of an emergency, especially at Mass. One was known as the Buttock Clench.

When the dangers of pollution threatened to disrupt the Mass, they became immobile, instantly statuesque. They then performed a swallowing motion with the inner ring to contain the offensive gas. And, finally, to seal off any escape, the buttocks would be tightened into a clenched ball.

The Bouncing Method involved standing on the balls of the feet. The timing had to be perfect to achieve total anonymity. When bouncing harmoniously to each hymn, a salvo of short, sharp bursts could be fired by clapping the buttocks together – phutt, phutt, phutt – Amen.

BRRRRRRRRRRRRRRRRRRRRR-P – 'Fuckin pea soup,' a voice whispered.

Barney let himself drift into the warmth of his shawl, and sleep. Content now that the plan had been hatched, he could rest up – 'Nightyho eh.'

Chapter Six

THE MARYLAND IS dark inside. The cloud of smoke hanging in the air reeks of cannabis. Jake and Skud don't fit in with the audience of long hair, beards and beads, but seem unaware of the malicious vibe they give off. People quietly move away as the two make their way towards the stage, but they don't notice: they're quite accustomed to people moving away. There are five different heavy rock bands playing a live concert. Both Jake and Skud want to be near the stage – 'Here, Jake! S'like bein at that concert at Woodstock!' Skud shouts amid the roaring guitars howling and wa-wa-ing through his ears: he rocks back and forward to the beat pounding against his chest like waves, his hair lashing his face – 'MAAAAN! F-U-C-K-I-N BRULLIAAANT! MAAAAN!'

Jake nods coolly, conscious of the wary eyes upon him. He enjoys the power of being dangerous, feels that adrenalin shooting through his body, his arm twitching to reach for the invisible guitar, but he knows he's being watched so remains ice cool, slightly swaying; the hypnotic pulse of the sounds taking hold of his being, pulling him into a rhythm with the flow of swaying hippies sitting cross-legged on the floor, or leaning against the surrounding walls, concealing one-skinner joints, or gathered in a smaller tribe doing blow-backs, and shouting – 'FAR OUT! MAAAAN! YEAH MAAAAN!'

During the brief interlude between the bands they feel other eyes bearing down upon them – clear, sober eyes. Jake lacerates the audience with a cold perusal. One or two appear to be playing at a private concert, waving their hair wildly to a totally different beat, the invisible guitars wa-wa-ing soundlessly, others are simply sitting back listening to the bands, beards hanging open, eyes half-closed. They all seem to be in a trance, smiling and grinning. Jake just can't make it out. They all know something. Something he and Skud don't know. That smiling, like they're sharing some magical secret or something. Is it drugs, he wonders? He's about to concede that it must be dope that is making them all happy when he detects the source of the sober eyes. They belong to three guys and a bird. They glance away when he meets their eyes, but he keeps catching them staring at him. There's something about them. Their body language is all wrong. They're seemingly stoned, but somehow they don't look wrecked. He can't put his finger on it, but there's something not right about them.

Skud responds to the nudge in the ribs and looks over at them – 'They cunts starin at us?' he asks.

Jake shrugs – 'Fuck knows. Here, check the gear thur wearin,' he replies.

Their carefully disarranged look clashes with the bearded wrecks around them. Their combat jackets, the ban-the-bomb signs on the back, and the tee shirts, they're too clean-looking, and all that shit on the front – Turn On Chill Out, Peace and Love, Pink Floyd and Che Guevara.

Skud shouts at them with a maniacal look in his eyes – 'MAAAN!'

Jake blatantly scrutinises them. Their hair, not short, but not long. Catalogue hippies, he thinks. They're probably trying to score, he smiles. There was something just not right about them. Then he tipples what it is. The smiling – they're not smiling.

'V'ye goat that blade oan ye, Skud? S'cunts urny stoned. Get a cuppla pints,' he orders.

Skud swaggers towards the tiny bar at the back of the club, snarling as he passes the four bogus hippies.

'MAAAAAN!' They deliberately look in another direction, failing to notice his hand beneath his shirt.

'FUCKIN BAMS!' he barks in their faces, hoping to provoke them into a response, but again they look elsewhere.

'MAAAAAN!' He bangs the bar top – 'Here! Two pintsa heavy, pal! Fuckin Osmands o'er er eh,' he laughs.

A tap on the shoulder has him whirling round, his hand tightly gripping the handle of the steak knife, as he almost springs upon the unseen appendage.

'Whu? Fucksake, man! S'you! Dawn!' he laughs in relief – 'Thought that wis some bampot there. Aw here, check ye oot, man,' he says sweeping her off her feet in a hug – 'Ye missed me then? Listen, fore ye say anathin. Av been oot graftin wi Jake an Barney. We dun a turn but the coppers dug us up, battured the cunts.'

Dawn throws her head back, her long blonde hair cascading down her back, close to her waistline. Blue intelligent eyes search her man's.

'Aw, Skud. Noa again. Ye oan the run? Much didye get fae the turn?' she asks.

Skud pushes her back against the bar, grinding his hips against her long legs – 'Turn it up. Here, stick this in yer bag tae we get ootside,' he says, slipping the steak knife into her hand – 'C'mere, am burstin fur ma hole,' he whispers as he tongues her ear.

Dawn pushes at him, giggling – 'Stoap it, ya fuckin bampot. People kin see us.'

Skud glances over his shoulder, grinning stupidly – 'Fuck thum. Listen, am gettin us a quartera black. Ye like black, eh? Good fur ridin, eh? Where we stayin the night?'

Dawn pulls her cheesecloth top back into place, tucking it into her jeans – 'Look you, that's the only time you want ey see me, when yer horny,' she teases.

Skud pushes her legs apart with his knee; he feels the bulge of that pussy against his thigh – 'Oh, Jesus. C'mon, turn it up, ye know av goat feelins fur ye. A don't go aboot wi urra burds, dae ah? C'mon, where wi stayin, am burstin tae ride ye, c'mon eh, it's me, yer man,' he pleads.

Dawn knows he's hooked, but for how long she can't imagine – 'Okay. Angie's huvin a blaw later so we kin go up tae hur hoose. S'that Jake wi ye?' she asks.

Skud indicates over his shoulder – 'Aye, how?' he asks.

She shakes her head – 'Naw, nae chance. He freaks everybody oot. Angie hates the guy. Tryin tae dae es Charles Bronson. Thinks es in *Death Wish*. Want's tae get es fuckin act thegither. A think es a poof.'

Skud's face changes – 'Wit? Wit ye fuckin talkin boot? Jake's bran new. Es ma best mate, ya cunt. Fuck Angie. Opens ur mooth an she'll get battured. Wit?'

Dawn feels his arms fall away from her – 'Well, a mean es never goat a burd has ey?' she explains, dropping her head to stare at the floor knowingly.

She feels the clip on the chin as he flicks her head back with his fingers 'Listen you. Wan mer fuckin word an al punch ye aw o'er this fuckin place. Dae ye hear me?' his voice hisses – 'Eh? Did ye fuckin hear me?' he demands, clipping her again.

Dawn nods her head, but remains silent in an act of defiance.

She feels another clip on the chin, harder this time, but refuses, still, to let him see the tears welling up, or her hurt. She flinches when she feels his hand clamp around her windpipe, pulling her face up to meet his wild eyes, and seething warnings spewing out from his bared teeth – 'Av telt ye afore. Don't get fuckin wide, hen. Am fuckin warnin ye.'

She smirks as he throws her back against the bar, drawing him a look of contempt to let him know that she isn't afraid of him – 'Stupit fuckin cow,' he sneers – 'Al get that message ootside. An Jake's cumin way me.'

Dawn watches him push past people – 'Fuckin bampot,' she laughs – 'Lookit um. The fuckin bampot.'

Skud swings on the combat jackets as he pushes past them, deliberately spilling beer over their feet – 'Shamrock ya bass! Ya fuckin rides!' he leers – 'MAAAAN!'

Jake takes his pint – 'They fuckin sayin?' he asks indicating with his head in the direction of the foursome – 'S'that Dawn at the bar?'

Skud shakes his head in frustration – 'They cunts? Ach, nuthin man, ye kiddin. Aye, a told ur tae fuck off. Fuckin wumin, man! Dae yer fuckin box in, man. The band's back oan in a minut.'

Jake agrees – 'Aye eh. Fuckin wumin, man. Cunts.'

Skud laughs – 'Disnae matter wit ye dae fur thum, the cunts. R'always fuckin moanin aboot sum fuckin thing. Cunts.'

BWAM! BWAM! BWAM! BWAM! A sudden burst of drums and throbbing bass guitar throws the audience into a frenzy of grinning as one of those old familiar numbers is slammed into their rib cages – Jimi Hendrix's 'Purple Haze'. Skud explodes into a wild Apache dance, tearing off his shirt, and landing amongst the acid freaks, swaying their hair back and forward as they acknowledge some personal tribute to a trip experienced in a previous happening. Jake watches in amusement as the knowing looks connect with the broadening grins of those old Sixties members of the former flower power colony. The only thing expanding here are the daft grins, he thinks. He feels the adrenalin rushing through him as the bass guitar number bites at his brain with those two powerful chords, but he remains still. He laughs when those knowing we-know-something-you-don't-know looks ripple through the faces, as the lead singer blurts out – 'S'cuse me while ah kiss this guy!' followed by the inevitable roars of – 'YEAH MAAAAN! FAR OUT MAAAAN! YEAAAAH!'

Skud shouts in his ear as the number ends – 'AM GONNY GET SOME DOPE. WANTA PINT WHILE AM UP?'

Jake nods – 'Aye, nae borra.'

Skud lurches towards the toilet to find some dope. The days when hippies wanted to simply 'turn on' people with free dope and acid were long gone. Drugs brought in a few quid. Guaranteed invites to parties, lots of nice pussy, but the price phenomena is the 'happening' of these times. Still, there exists a breed accustomed to paying for nothing, particularly shit like acid and cannabis. Well, let's face it. Who is going to pay five quid for a tiny piece of cardboard with some logo identifying it as an experience in California Sunshine, Strawberry Fields or Black Microdot?

Skud could have a party with a fiver and still have enough for a fish supper. Acid and Blaw? They were free as far as he was concerned. There was no way he was paying for that crap, especially some stupid longhair. He simply took, and that was that. The jail? Jail was an inevitable part of life. He could handle jail; most of his pals from the old gang days were doing time. He didn't mind the odd sixer. Sometimes it's the only way he can see old pals. There are occasional square-gos sometimes, but there's no bad blood between rival gangs. Acid, hash and fucking. All in that order. That's how it is. Robberies take a dive. Balaclavas are hidden. Everybody's chilled out.

There's Jake and Skud though. Seventies Sykos. Acid, blades and fucking is more their line of thought.

Skud's violent vibe permeates the toilet like tentacles reaching behind the acid-filled dilated pupils of longhairs looking for a quarter to take to the next tepee – 'S'happenin, man?' he asks, pointing his prick at the urinal, smiling over his shoulder.

An Afghan coat is standing in a cubicle selling dope; the strip of acid tabs hangs from his sleeve – 'V'got tabs, man. Black Microdot, man. Yeah man, s'cool man. S'beautiful, man. Trippy stuff, man. Av got black tae. Twenty-eight quid an ounce. Daen quarters as well man, aw yeah, man, quality shit, man, good shit, man.'

Skud shoves his prick away as he swaggers the few feet to the cubicle. He leans into the frame, stretching his muscles – 'Much ye goat, pal?' he grins.

The queue of moccasins and sandals pick up the vibes screeching off the tiles as one of their own is cornered and about to be brought down by the worst imaginable trip through the myriad of avenues in the hallucinogenic-friendly toilet frame.

'Many tabs?'

The fur coat shimmers.

Skud takes the brother in his arms – 'Bet your name's Jesus, innit?' he leers – 'Meetra Devul!' He grips a bony arm as he pulls the longhair back over the toilet bowl – 'Get the fuckin lot oot, son. C'mon, that's it. Peace, man. Don't want ripped, dae ye? S'it pal, get the lot oot. Much is er aw thegither, MAAAAN?' he asks.

The Devil? Ripped? The threat howls through the tribe staring through the walls over the urinal; piss becomes trapped in bowels as dicks take fright and cause a traffic jam at the door: there're free flights beyond the sweating torso breathing bad vibes, but it's dangerous terrain to cross while the deranged meets a hallucinogenic in the formerly known state of flower power.

'Two-hunner tabs, man. Thur noa mine man. Honest, a only sell man. Oh please, don't hurt me, man, please, bad trip, man. Here, thur's four ounsa black, don't touch me, man, please man, man please, nae vialence man, plea—'

'S'CUSE ME WHILE AH KISS THIS GUY'

Skud leans back — 'Aw far oot, man,' he mocks, pocketing the black and the acid. He emerges from the cubicle, grinning — 'FAR FUCKIN OOT, MAAAAN!'

Jake shrugs when he returns — 'Where ye been? Dope? Aye, right. Goan get two mer pints. S'nearly finished. Last band's comin oan,' he drawls.

Skud sees Dawn and Angie. They both look down their noses at him as he walks over to the bar — 'You'se two cunts lookin at?' he hisses.

Dawn laughs — 'Daen yer tea boy again?' she taunts.

Skud blanks the burst of giggling — 'Two pints, pal, an two Carlsberg Specials. Aye, fur the two pigs,' he says, nodding towards the two birds.

Angie smiles from behind long jet-black hair — 'Thanks, Skud. Ye noa talkin tae Dawn? Am huvin a blaw later, ye's kin come up, thurs a bed.'

Dawn dances lazily before him as he delivers their beer, but looks up as he pushes the lump of blaw into her hand – 'Here. Stick that in yer bag. Ye's want acid tabs? Black Micradot.'

Angie clocks the dope – 'Fucksake man! Where d'ye get that? S'black tae. Aw Skud yer a big darlin, so ye ur. Dawn, look,' she squeals.

Dawn feels Skud's prick pressing against her as she dances in between them, waving that long hair in his face. She doesn't notice the lump of cellophane he bites off before he pushes the remainder of the acid strip into her hand – 'Here. Take that tae. Punt sum tae they daft longhairs.'

Angie laughs as she sees the effect of her pal's dancing – 'Whoooof! Dawn, lookit that fuckin thing! Whoooo-oooo-ooo!' she giggles, pointing down at his fly.

Skud swaggers away, delighted with himself – 'See ye's ootside, hen. Angie. Talk tae that fuckin nutcase wull ye. Fuckin bust ur if she keeps gettin wide,' he laughs.

Dawn finally draws him a glance accompanied with a slight half-smile – 'Aye ye gonny bust me the night then?' She has him by the balls – 'Skud?'

He grunts as he sees those hips for a moment grinding wildly over his shoulder – 'Aw, Jesus.'

Jake takes his pint – 'Hanks. S'Dawn sayin? That Angie way ur?' he asks – 'Love tae pump that wee cow.'

Skud hesitates for a moment but then laughs – 'Aye. Dae ur the night. Huvin a blaw a think. Ye comin up tae ur hoose? C'mon Jake,' he pleads.

Jake nods – 'Aye, might aswell, fuck all else tae dae.'

Skud's elated – 'YES! Here. Ye want sum acid, Jake? Av jist dun a bit. Ye sure?' he asks.

Jake has no interest in mind expansion unless it's with a

hatchet – 'Acid? Ye kiddin? Many didye take? Feel enahin yet?' he asks.

Skud shrugs his shoulders – 'How many? Wit ye talkin aboot? A jist swallied it. How ye supposed tae count thum?'

Jake looks at him curiously – 'You gettin wide? D'ye swallie a whole strip? R'you aff yer heid? You've dun yer skull, man. S'Dawn know? This'll be a fuckin laugh. Here. Av heard ye kin see elephants an that wi the fuckin stuff, man.'

Hill Street looks like a biblical gathering with long hair and beards searching the night starscape for signs of the next coming, but the focus of the dilated pupils is dope, and a floor to camp on until the next happening – 'Maaaan. Yeah, man. Dealers here. He was here, man. Saw the man in the toilet, man. Yeah, maaaan. Cool. YEAH, MAAAAN. HEEEY! How ya doin, maaaan? MAAAAN!'

There's nothing worse than a Glasgow accent trying to sound American – 'MAAAAAAAN'

Skud and Jake's presence intensifies the atmosphere as they emerge from the club to look for Dawn and Angie – 'The fuck ur they two cunts?'

No one dares say where for fear of inviting trouble.

Dawn and Angie have become engaged with the ban-the-bomb movement – 'S'that a real mustash?' Angie asks the combat jacket as they are leaving.

The Starsky lookalike looks into her brown eyes – 'Yeah man.' he smiles at the black eyelash flash – 'That chic wi you? We're tryin tae score, man,' he smiles.

Dawn draws him a look – 'A wit? A chic? Aw, here. Chase yer self, son. A chic. D'ye think yer in the movies, son?' She nudges Angie – 'A chic? Fuckin Bovril, eh. Score? Should send thum tae they urra two bampots,' she giggles.

Angie's snigger seems empty – 'Aye, a know.' She digs her elbow into her pal.

'Och, Dawn. He wis nice!' she complains – 'Ad a shagged um. Aye, too right. S'awright fur you innit, noa wit a mean?'

Dawn smirks – 'Och. Shag anythin, so ye wid. Lookit thum. Jake fancies ye anyway.'

Angie screams in mock protest – 'Wit? Jake? Aye, right. He's stone fuckin mad. Geez me the creeps wi they eyes. Fuckin Charles Manson. Aw here, don't tell me.'

Dawn stops further protest – 'C'mon Angie. Av noa seen um fur weeks. Jake'll leave. Ey hates hash, makes um para. Anyway, ey likes you Angie.'

Angie looks back inside – 'Wers that guy? Kin ye see um? Kin invite thum up. Skud wullny bother. Oh, there ey is.' She waves at him – 'Oh, Dawn, ey winked at me.'

Dawn looks at her resignedly – 'Better noa call me a chic in front ey Skud. Ye know wit es like. Am tellin ye. Es tooled right up. N'that fuckin Jake.'

Angie can think of only one tool at a time, the one smiling at her – 'Aye, okay. Al keep thum in the scullery tae you's two go tae bed, okay?'

Dawn sighs – 'Aye, okay. Fuck, lookit um tae. Right. Al go an get Skud.' She says it with some reservation – 'S'your hoose. Kin ye see they two?'

Jake's hanging over the railing outside the club – 'Fucksake man,' he spits as a vomit flow erupts from his belly – 'Fuckin ulcers.'

Skud screams suddenly as an orgasmic shudder ripples

through his body – 'ARGHHH! JESUS CHRIST MAN! DIDYE HEAR THAT?'

Jake's looking at him – 'S'at? Hear wit?' he asks.

Skud's eyes are like flying saucers – 'Ma ears! Ma fuckin ears, man! A heard thum er! They slapped right aff ma fuckin skull! D'ye noa hear thum, Jake?'

Jake drops his head – 'Aye, righvwoooouuuuppppp! Vwoooouuuuupppppppppppppp!'

Skud catches the vomit cascading in slow motion from his partner's head – 'The fucks that Jake?' he asks giggling – 'S'that fuckin stuff. Ohhh here, wit the fucks happenin man? A feel fuckin weird here. Here? Jake, where the fuck ur wi man?'

Jake leans back – 'S'the matter wi you noo?' he snaps.

Skud's bouncing up and down – 'MAAAN! HAAW! HAAW! HAAW! FUCKIN MENTAL!' he howls into the night – 'FUCK-IN MENT-AAAL YA BASS! SHAMROCKKKKKKK!' KKKKKKKKKKKKKKKCORMAHS! The roar bounces back off a wall – 'FUCK! JAKE! WATCH THIS, MAN! SHAM-ROCKKKKKKKKKKK!' KKKKKKKKKKCORMAHS! – 'Did ye see that? Fuckinhell! Maan! A kin see words man! Jake, check, man! HERE YOU!' UOY EREH! bounces right back at him – 'D'ye hear it? AOOOUUUUWWWW! AOOOUUUUWWWW! AOOOUUUUWWWW!'

Dawn hears the howl too – 'Who the fuck is that?'

The crowd scatters to expose her man there in the middle of the street howling like a wolf – 'AOOOUUUUWWWWW! AOOOUUUUWWWW! AOOOUUUUWWWW!'

Jake's laughing as she comes over – 'S'he daen, Jake? Fuckin steamur.'

Angie takes her arm – 'Oh, Jesus Christ. Check Skud, Dawn,' she giggles.

Skud's broken into an Indian war dance – 'HUYA! HUYA! HUYA!'

Dawn pulls at Jake – 'Goan get him fur fucksake, you.'

Skud looks fearsome, sweat running down his bare chest. No one will go near him as he squares the circle of onlookers. Most of them know what's happening anyway. He is a genie creeping up the spout to wreak havoc on reality. A ripple of energy surging out through his pores almost lifts him off his feet – 'Awww here, mannn.'

He feels the super force rush through his prick; he has it out for the crowd to observe the true meaning of Purple Haze – 'Check this fuckin thing mannn. Awwww fuckkkk.' The stunned sensibilities around him can't take their eyes off it as he begins to slowly stroke the huge stump – 'Awww mannnn. The Huggy Monstur. Check it oot. S'Moby Dick.'

Jake finally makes a move – 'Here you, ya fuckin bam. C'mon, Dawn's fuckin rajin man, fur fucksake,' he says pulling him over to the two birds.

Dawn turns her face away indignantly – 'Fuckin bam, so ye ur. S'the fuckin matter wi you eh?' she asks.

Skud's beyond the logic of reason, beyond their perceptions – gone – 'S'the wit? That me that said that? Kin you hear wit am thinkin? Lookit your eyes man.' His thought processes are disintegrating into a mass of disconnected fragments, breaking through the psychological framework that protects him from being hit by a bus – 'Mannnn,' he groans sensually – 'Ma hole, mannn.'

Angie's beside Dawn – 'Many pints did ey huv?' she asks – 'Oh Dawn, look. There es comin o'er, that guy wi the mustash. Al ask um noo. Who's that way um? Look, thur must be aboot eight ey thum. They canny aw come. Here they come. S'ma hair look awright, Dawn?'

Jake finishes pissing in a doorway just as the others are surrounded by more haircuts and combat jackets – 'Who the fucks that?' he wonders.

Skud's becoming disassociated with language – 'The who? Drug Squad? S'this fuckin bampot talkin aboot?' he asks the others, laughing – 'The who?'

Dawn's heard of them but thought they were just a rumour – 'Leave him alane, you. A don't gie a fuck who ye ur. Get yer fuckin hauns aff ma man.'

Skud's laughing; the head-butt that flashed through his brain failed to co-ordinate with his forehead – 'Kin you hear wit am thinkin, pal?' he asks, breaking into hysterics. He pulls his arms free – 'Hauns aff, pal. Noa tell ye again. Aye, a wull. Hauns AFF! HAW! HAW! HAW! Get it? Hauns aff?'

A lined face floats before his psychedelic vision – 'Detective Sergeant Leslie Brown of Strathclyde Region. I'm charging you with trafficking under the—'

Skud's in hysterics – 'Traffic? A canny fuckin drive!'

The face persists – 'Under the Drugs Act . . . Under the . . . I'm charging yo . . .'

Skud draws a breath – 'AOOOUUUUWWWW! Check that haircut man! S'Adolf Hitlur!' he roars – 'SEIG HEIL! SEIG HEIL! SEIG HEIL! ACHTUNG! JAKE! JAKE! WAIT TAE YE SEE THIS MOB! THE DRUG SQUAD. V'YE GOAT SOME DRUGS? HERE TAKE AW TIIIS. AL GET MER PAL. YE'S WANTY COME TAE A WEE PARTY WI US?'

Jake's watching from the doorway – 'Coppers?' The two panda cars that screech onto the pavement convince him that they are police – 'Fucksake man.'

Skud screeches – 'HERE YOU!' Terror claws at his heart. His woman is being pushed into a van – 'THE FUCK YE DAEN? LEAVE HUR, YA PRICK!' he screams.

A combat jacket goes sprawling into the middle of the road as an explosion of energy erupts in the midst of the police. BANG! Another's felled, but there're too many. Skud is barely controllable. He's struggling with five of them. Their batons are out – BANG! BANG! They batter his skull – 'A belt! Get him intae a belt!' a voice is shouting. He doesn't feel the pain, but watches from a distance as the blows strike tiny sparks over his head and body each time they land – 'AOOOUUUUWWWWW! AOOOUUUUWWWW! AOOOUUUUWWWWW!' a voice howls through the night.

Jake fades into the darkness. His partner having been carted to the jail, he decides to lie low until morning – 'Bastards.' He prowls the streets until he comes across what he's looking for, an old derellict tenement. The hideout provides shelter from the wind collecting newspapers and other trash lying around. After breaking down the door for firewood he hunkers down in a corner and watches the sparks explode across the old bare floorboards. He lights a cigarette, and watches the long tails peeping from their holes – 'Shooda went tae the movies,' he thinks aloud – '*Fist Fulla Dollars.*'

Barney's face flits up before his eyes. Two pals in the jail he thinks to himself. What the fuck's happened? Had the Pakis coppered them up? It was a possibility, but they wouldn't have known where to look for them. No, it had to be that blonde. She must have grassed. This is all her fault he decides – 'Fuckpig. Poor fuckin Skud.'

*   *   *

Sixteen hours later there's a howl from the DT Tank in Barlinnie Prison Hospital Wing – 'AOOOUUUUWWWWW! AOOOUUUUWWWW! AOOOUUUUWWWW!'

Skud's lying in the middle of the floor. Life's big deal has just risen from the dead like Lazarus – 'Aw, Dawnnnn,' he groans, unable to stroke the huge mushroom poking up a tent under his new canvas smock – 'A luv ye, darlin.'

Two prison doctors observing him through the reinforced glass window look at each other – 'So what do you think?' They agree that it might be in his own interest to section him as a cautionary measure under the Mental Health Act for twenty-four hours – 'Yes, he's a danger to himself as well as other people. Woodilee Hospital? What about testing his IQ? Still seems disorientated.'

Skud's brought before the doctors in the surgery interview room – 'Bit tied up here, eh boss,' he laughs, nodding at the restraint belt – 'Dun fur pickin ma nose man.'

The doctor interviewing him smiles while his colleague observes the patient from the seat in the corner. He looks down at the sheet of paper on the table – 'Now, this is all a fairly simple process. Can you tell me what day this is?' he asks.

Skud laughs – 'Aw c'mon, don't start. This a quiz?'

The doctor ticks a mark in a box – 'Do you know what day this is?' he persists.

Skud gets the idea – 'Aw right, a see. Eh, Friday? Naw haud oan, Wedn . . . ?' he asks.

The doctor smiles – 'Fine. Can you tell me the name of the Queen?'

Skud frowns – 'The Queen? Queen? Freddie Mercury, dae ye mean?'

The doctor looks up from the paper – 'Tell me. Who is the current Prime Minister?'

Skud shifts around in his seat – 'S'that him wi the pipe? Harry ur sumthin?'

The doctor smiles again – 'Did you vote in the last general election?' he asks.

Skud's bamboozled – 'The wit? Kin ye repeat the question, wisnae ready there,' he smirks – 'The general wit?'

The doctor leans back, fiddling with the pencil in his mouth – 'Mr O'Hara. Define right from wrong, will you?'

Skud laughs – 'Aw c'mon man, these ur aw fuckin trick questions. Right. Who scored the second in the Scottish Cup wi Celtic an Rangers? Aye, see! C'mon then! Al gie ye clue. Witsat?' he asks, looking over his shoulder.

Two warders in white medic coats move in to escort him back to the tank. Skud bows to the doctor – 'Right, Bamber. Nice meetin ye. Back tae the fish tank, eh? Umma noa gettin a prize? Aw they questions? By the way, ye's wur cheatin. The Queen's name? Aye, right. S'Betty innit. Prime thingmy? Winston Churchull winnit? See! A knew aw the time. HAUW! HAUW! HAUW!'

The two doctors look at each other, bemused by the befuddled – 'Doesn't know what planet he's on. Have him moved to Woodilee. Inform the courts in the morning. Take him straight from the Sheriff Court. Fine then.'

They smile at the call of the wild – 'Dearie me.'

'AOOUUWWW! AOOUUWWW! AOOUUWWW!'

Chapter Seven

THE SHERIFF COURT holding cells are bulging from the weekend lie downs. McGinty has been down there for two days, but bail's been set by his lawyer and the PF. Johnny is being taken upstairs when he sees Skud – 'Hauw! Skud!' He's being held in the cage for capital charges; murderers and head cases – 'Ye dun fur?' he shouts.

Skud sits staring ahead with a malicious smile across his face – 'How ye doin, Johnny. Ach, a loada shite. Dun fur a chibbin. Copper up in the Woodside. Tell Jake tae see Dawn. Am pleadin tae the lot so mind and tell thum. Like ma belt? HAUW! HAUW!' he laughs – 'Sein the jail sykie the s'efternin.'

Johnny looks back – 'Nae bother, mate. Ye okay?'

Skud looks up with a glint in his eye – 'AOOOUUUWWW! AOOOUUUWWWW! HUYA! HUYA! HUYA!'

Auld Santa Claus looks at the accused standing before him in the restraint belt – 'Do I know you, young man?' he asks before remanding him.

Skud's brief puts forward a plea – 'Your Honour, it is my understanding that my client is to be detained. We therefore make no application for bail to be fixed at this stage. I believe that matters currently under investigation by the police may indeed be—'

Santa interrupts the young lawyer – 'Yes, yes, yes. Does Mr O'Hara understand these proceedings are to—'

Skud interrupts the court – 'HUYA! HUYA! HUYA!'

He's still howling as the police drag him from the dock past the public gallery where a familiar face is stunned in disbelief. Dawn is sitting with Angie. McGinty is watching the performance from the back of the court.

'Jesus. S'dun es fuckin box,' he says as they all meet on the street – 'The fuck happened?'

Dawn shakes her head – 'Aw, fur fucksake. Acid, Johnny. Took some acid last night up at the Maryland. How'd you get on?'

Johnny laughs – 'Fifty-quid bail. Acid? Much did ey take, man?' he asks.

Dawn doesn't know – 'Fuck knows. Wit happens noo? How dae a see um?'

Johnny shrugs his shoulders – 'Woodilee, hen. Nuthoose. Jist phone an say ye wanta visit pass tae see yer man, tell thum ye's ur merried.'

Angie giggles, whispering – 'They huv dances in there, Dawn. Ye kin get yer thingamy jigged, know wit a mean?'

Dawn looks at her – 'You serious? D'ye think am gaun in there tae drap ma knickers? Ye aff yer heid? Imagine him at a dance?' she sneers.

Johnny agrees – 'Better than they fuckin cells. Al fuckin tell ye that,' he laughs – 'Ma fuckin heid's nippin, man. Listen. Av still got a few quid, ye's fancy the George?'

Dawn and Angie are undecided – 'Ach, eh. D'ye fancy, Angie? Am noa bothered.'

Angie squeals suddenly – 'Thanks, Johnny, eh. Dawn, listen. We'll come up later, okay? Av a wee message furst. See ye up there. Dawn, c'mere quick,' she blurts out.

Dawn digs her in the ribs – 'S'that aw aboot? Thoat ye fancied him?'

Angie blushes – 'Tampax! Ma period's jist started. Kin ye smell anathin?' she tries to whisper – 'Jesus, thuv jist started. Kin he smell enathin? Oh. Fuck. S'terrible innit?'

Dawn throws her head back, laughing – 'Och, Angie. Smell fish, Johnny?'

Angie's squealing – 'Dawn! S'terrible! Johnny, don't listen tae hur. Dawn! S'terrible, so it is! Right. Listen, am away the noo. Al catch ye's up there,' she says, marching off to the nearest chemist – 'N'Dawn! Don't tell him anythin. Right?'

Dawn's laughing – 'Och. Don't worry. Wait. Al come way ye,' she calls after her.

Johnny looks confused – 'Fish?' he asks – 'Ach, listen, al see ye's up there.' He turns to cross the road but remembers the message – 'Oh. A meant tae tell ye. Skud says es pleadin guilty so yev tae impeach um fur the blade an the dope. Right, am headin up the road. Al wait fur ye's up there, okay?'

Dawn nods – 'Aye, but wit's ey bein dun wi? Jist a bitta dope? They charged me wi the blade in ma bag. Am oot oan fuckin bail. S'that wit ey means?'

Johnny shrugs his shoulders – 'A don't know. Jist passin oan the message,' he says.

Angie tugs at Dawn's sleeve – 'Dawn, c'mon. C'mon eh, please?' she sniffs.

Dawn laughs – 'Right, right am comin. Wull cross o'er here.'

They try to cross the busy street, but their path is blocked; the police van leaving from the back entrance of the court is rolling from side to side as the sole passenger waves good-bye – 'AOOOUUUUWWWW! AOOOUUUUWWWW! AOOOUUUUWWWW!'

Dawn stares – 'Aw, don't tell me.'

Johnny grins – 'Skud, eh.'

Sanji is about to have tea when there's a knock at the door – 'Who's that?' he wonders, getting up from the table – 'Postman's already been.'

Rashid jumps when he hears the voices – 'Mr Patel? I'm afraid I have some bad news. There's been an unfortunate accident . . . May we come in?'

Sanji guides the two uniformed police officers into the main dining-room.

'I'm sorry, I don't know what you mean,' he says, confused – 'Saab Patel? Ye-es, he is my brother. Whatt? Dead? Are you serious, sir?'

The young officer removes his hat and sits down – 'Am afraid so. He was found in the early hours of this morning. A post mortem will be carried out and a report will be made to the Procurator Fiscal's office. At this point in time there's not much can be done, to be honest, other than identification,' says the officer. 'Would it be possible for a member of the family to come down to the station? There are some, eh, personal belongings, and a senior officer may wish to speak with you. I'm extremely sorry, sir.' He adds – 'There's not much more we can say at this point.'

Sanji stares at the floor, stunned – 'Oh, sorry, sorry, I . . .' he apologises – 'I'll come down myself,' he stammers – 'Only, could I . . . Could I tell my family first? My mother's, very very old and . . .'

The two officers get to their feet – 'Oh, not at all, sir,' they reply, keen to leave – 'Could you call in later today then, sir? I'm sure you will want to speak with someone, there's the desk sergeant. He may want to help. Anyway . . .'

Rashid re-appears when the front door closes – 'Sanji? Wit wis that?' he asks – 'Saab deid? S'that wit ey said there?'

Sanji is staring at the floor in silence.

'Sanji?' repeats his brother – 'Te-ll me. Wit did they say there aboot Saab?' he asks, his voice breaking – 'Is Saab deid?'

The older brother wrings his hands – 'Ra,' he says quietly – 'Get Mother down. She's upstairs, she has to be told . . .' He adds – 'Saab is dead.'

Rashid does as he's told without question – 'Right, Sanji, al get ur,' he whimpers – 'Ma brother . . .'

Mrs Patel throws her hands in the air and starts wailing. Glasgow, they should never have come to this place, she cries. Their father had promised to take them all home after the war. This is all his fault, she wails. Her sons had been corrupted by this terrible country, they did not belong here. – 'Take us home, Sanji! Take us home to Pakistan!'

Both Sanji and Rashid hold her – 'Oh Mother, please,' pleads the older brother – 'What can I do?' he cries – 'What can I do?'

Together, they rock back and forth on the settee for almost an hour before the woman has to be taken to her bed.

'Ra,' snivels Sanji – 'We have to talk.'

Rashid drops his head. How could his brother be dead? he asks himself. How? Only yesterday they had been laughing and joking, and now he was gone?

He holds his head in his hands – 'Sanji. Wit ur wi gonny dae?' he pleads – 'Saab dun nuthin n noo es deid, ma big bro-ther, deid,' he cries – 'N'wit aboot me? Wit's gonny happen tae me? Sanji,' he sobs – 'Wit's gonny happen? N'wit about Saab . . . ?'

Sanji takes his brother by the shoulders – 'Oh, Rashid I know son, I know,' he says – 'I promise to look after you,' he swears – 'I'll look after you now.'

Rashid turns to him – 'But how did ey die?' he asks – 'How, Sanji?'

Sanji shakes his head – 'They don't know yet, an accident,' he replies – 'Look, Rashid, I'll find out, then I think we should talk, decide what to do.' He tries to explain.

'Thur no takin me away, Sanji!' interrupts his distraught brother – 'Thur no takin me tae that station, am tellin ye, Sanji!'

Sanji rubs his brother's head – 'No, Rashid, they're not taking you away, but we have to talk later.'

Rashid pushes his brother's hand away – 'Naw! Am tellin ye!' he shouts – 'Thurs nae point talkin. Saab's deid n am no gaun near that fuckin place! So ye better no tell the cops anythin aboot me!'

Sanji tries to soothe him, but he's hysterical—

'Naw, Sanji!' he snaps, wiping his nose clean – 'Look, thurs nae point. Thull be waitin fur me.'

Sanji nods, defeated – 'I know, Rashid,' he agrees – 'I know, son, but listen first. Saab has to be identified,' he states – 'I'll go down to the station on my own, okay? No, no . . . Listen to me,' he pleads – 'You look after Mother. Right? And I'll go down there and find out what happened to Saab. Okay? Then we can talk about what to do? Please, Rashid, is that okay?'

'Right Sanji, but am tellin ye, am no stayin here. Am takin ma maw tae Pakistan. You kin stay here if ye want but am no gaun tae the jail. Ma maw's gonny need wanny us anyway, so al go wi ur tae Pakistan.'

They sit together for a moment, but the death has broken them forever. 'Right, Rashid, right, you go with her,' says Sanji – 'But let me just deal with our brother . . . We should bury him first before we do anything, okay?'

Rashid nods – 'Okay. But will you deal wi the cops? Poor Saab. A canny believe it. A mean, wit's happened?'

The George Hotel Bar is old cowboy hole-in-the-wall territory for the boys. Big Tam is an ex-copper, but he knows how to work the bar as manager without endangering his position with this crew. The same two-shilling piece on the bar has been passed back and forward to cover the pints since the Sixties. No money was ever exchanged. The Shamrock had fought coppers and gangs to rule the city centre. The Toon was theirs. You didn't fuck around with them, regardless of feather-cut hair-do's, beads and beards. They were still a team. Most were grafters and thieves, but there were the chib men too – cowboys.

McGinty glances over at the corner as he swaggers up to the bar – 'Lager, Tam. Jake, a pint?' he calls seeing the figure with his feet up on the table.

Jake looks up – 'Aye, how ye doin?' he asks.

Johnny pulls a chair up – 'Saw Skud. Dun es nut. Said tae tell ye. Es pleadin guilty tae the lot.'

Jake laughs – 'Took acid. Ye shooda seen um, Johnny. Right aff es fuckin heid. Daen a rain dance, up at the Maryland. Who's this drug squad by the way?' he asks.

Johnny raises his eyebrows – 'Aye, a heard. Here, ye wantey see um by the way. The DS? Drug Squad. Thur real coppers. How?' he queries.

Jake thinks back – 'That's who dun um. That fuckin daft

Angie. She wis talkin tae the cunts. Wit happened tae Dawn? She get snecked up tae?'

Johnny looks up – 'Saw Dawn at court, got bail. You ridin that wee Angie? Ye wanta anurra pint?'

Jake nods casually – 'Aye, might as well. See Auld Barney at court, Johnny?'

Johnny dumps the pints on the table – 'Aye. Walked last night.'

Jake sits up – 'Wit? Walked? Wit wis ey dun fur? We'd battured two coppers up the Woodside,' he complains – 'That auld cunt put es hauns up. Wit wis ey dun fur?'

Johnny shrugs – 'Forgeries. That Untouchable mob. A PF's release, slung.'

Jake frowns – 'Walked? Fuck. Ey hud a grand oan um aswell. Forgeries? Wit're ye talkin aboot, Johnny? Forgeries? Ey hud a grand oan um the auld cunt,' he states.

Johnny spills – 'Jake, am tellin ye. Watch wit yer daen wi him. Thur wis a Paki doon the cells. Gave Barney forgeries.'

Jake smiles viciously – 'Wit? Yer kiddin? They durty black bastards. Fuck sake man. Forgeries? N'Barney stull walks? Better noa huv pulled a move. Wit aboot Skud, eh? Right aff es fuckin heid, so ey is. Honest,' he says, shaking his head – 'Fuckin dancin. Prick oot tae, fuckin nutcase man.'

They both laugh into their pints – 'AOOUUUUWWWW!'

Dawn thinks she's hearing things as she walks into the bar – 'Jesus! The fuck's that? That you two?' she asks, looking round the corner.

Johnny hits the bar – 'Ye want tae drink, Dawn?'

Dawn takes a seat at the table – 'A Callie Special. Where've you been?' she asks the figure hunched in the corner.

Jake shrugs – 'Ye get bail, aye? D'ye see Skud? Say anathin

aboot me? A think Auld Barney mighta grassed us. Well, it looks at way. A PF's release? Fuck, r'ye kiddin?'

Dawn takes her drink – 'Hanks, Johnny. Angie's huvin a smoke later, f'ye wantey come up? Auld Barney grassed?' she asks.

Johnny grins – 'Magic, doll. Fuckin chokin fur a smoke, man. Whole weekend. Stuck doon they cells wi aw they fuckin bampots. Aye, time we gaun up?'

Dawn shakes her hair back – 'Ach, go up later. Cuppla Callie's furst. Where's this, eh, nuthoose? Woodilee Hospital, eh. Trust fuckin Skud,' she sighs.

Jake has other thoughts – 'Did Barney say anathin doon the cells? Mention me at aw? Say anathin aboot me? N'the cunt definitely walked?' he asks McGinty.

Johnny thinks – 'Na, nuthin. Wis jist the Paki. He wis doon the stairs wi me. Then av telt Barney. You there tae?' He gets the full picture now – 'Och, he's fuckin stuck you in, Jake. A PF's release? An es haudin the muney? S'a grass, that auld cunt.'

Jake doesn't need a lot of convincing, there has to be blame, a mouthpiece – 'Skud's jailed up tae? Na, am gonny look fur this auld bastard. Am tellin ye. How kin ye get oot efter gettin captured red-handed? Nah. Am takin the face aff um.'

Dawn takes another drink – 'Hanks, Johnny. How dae a get tae this place? S'a taxi go there?' she enquires before emptying the glass.

Johnny looks at her   'Fuckin Twilight Zone, eh. AOOOUUUUWWWW! Na, ye kin get a bus straight there,' he explains.

Dawn nods – 'D'ye hear that Angie gaun oan aboot thur dances? A fuckin headcase.'

Johnny laughs – 'Aye, Skud, eh. Shooda seen um doon they cells, howlin. S'Angie up the road by the way?'

Dawn remembers the smoke – 'Aye. She hud tae go a wee message. Wuv goat aboot three ounsa draw by the way. She'll gie ye a bit fur yersel. You cummin up, Jake?'

Johnny rubs hands – 'Right c'mon. Chokin fur a joint so am ur. Cummin up, Jake?'

Jake declines the offer to go with them for a smoke – 'Na, al see ye later. Tell Skud a wis askin fur um. Tell um al see that cunt Barney,' he says.

Dawn frowns – 'Listen, am noa sure aboot gaun tae this place. D'ye wantey go up tae visit wi me, Jake?'

Jake looks into his pint – 'Coppers might be lookin fur me, hen. S'nae point in the two ey us gettin the jail is thur.'

Dawn throws her hair back – 'Wit? Aw, c'mon. V'a got tae go up there masel? That's fuckin great, eh.'

Jake won't look at her – 'Jake, your es fuckin pal,' she snaps at him.

Johnny looks the other way. He doesn't want involved – 'Ye ready tae go, Dawn? he asks – 'M'dyin fura smoke.'

Dawn finishes her drink – 'Okay, Johnny. C'mon then.' She gets up from the table and goes to the toilet first – 'Noa be a minute. Get ye ootside.'

Johnny heads for the door – 'See ye later, Jake.'

Jake drains his pint – 'Aye, see ye later. Tell hur tae mind an tell Skud.'

Skud's beyond messages from the outside; travelling through the system from mildly ill to the wards of the severely, violently disturbed patients. Each day finds him slipping deeper and deeper into the size-fourteen slipper factory; his presence leaving bloody footprints, faces bearing the marks of a brief appearance on the wards for the canvas smocks until he finally arrives – The State Mental Hospital – 'AOOOUUUUWWWW!'

The Carstairs staff love him, his performance on a ward is unstoppable. They observe him take that bad trip down the highway of the insane; the first hallucinogenic disco dancer to take the floor on any ward. They watch this bad man fake himself over the edge of reason. His brain locked in fast-forward breakdown, permanent mental arrest in canvasville, at war with pyjama people – 'HERE YOUS CUNTS! AM SKUD!'

His face hits the happy smile club, the domino suite for killers and mass murderers on the road to nowhere – 'Chappin.' One patient, throwing lumps of shite at wire-meshed windows, looks up as an unfamiliar face covers himself in his mess – 'THE FUCK YOU LOOKIN AT?' screamed at him.

The patient's lips tremble – 'That's mine,' he dribbles.

Skud glares from the two holes of the hardening helmet – 'SHUT IT! RIGHT EN! WHO RUNS THIS FUCKIN PITCH?' he screams.

The patient grins – 'Big Haja,' he says.

Skud screens the ward of domino teams and wall scanners for the main man until he sees a head resembling a hand grenade – 'YOU TAJER? LIKE GENGHIS FUCKIN KHAN. GET THE PILLS AN FAGS OOT, YA FUCKIN BAMPOT YE!' he demands – 'C'MON EN!'

Big Haja has been on the ward for fifteen years; he's been living in limbo since killing a patient some years back, but his bubble is about to be burst, his reign of terror at an end, unless of course he can take this new guy out, catch him belted down in bed – 'A don't smoke. You've goat shite oan yer heid,' reply two black beady eyes from behind a hedge of eyebrows – 'Swallied ma pills s'mornin.'

The figure takes his position in the corner – 'THE MORRA!'

Skud progresses from leather belts to canvas jackets, peaking the most dangerous hit list, the heaviest dude in Carstairs. This becomes his life; fouling the food chain with spittal, keeping patients awake all night, every night, grinding them down to the bone before dragging them down like cattle in a spooked herd. He lives disconnected from the world, burning full throttle, leaving the mark of his ire, scorching a reputation as a crazy. To stop now would be to acknowledge this is not a joke, some bad trip – that he is fully committed, for life, a bovril – FAR OUT MAAAAN.

On his descent into madness he abandons all contact with the outside world; unfit for visits, unable to write letters, he drifts into complete isolation, cut off from everything but memories, fragments free-floating in a shuddering grey mess, trapped there in a bad happening called the Seventies.

When – 'YEAH MAAAAN,' became – 'HERE YOU CUNT!'

Life zooms past until his name accompanies 'D'ye mind?' – 'D'ye mind Skud?' The Jack Nicholson act's gone too far. It's not supposed to end like this. Where's the big Indian? No, this place is the dimension without any soundtrack; that same backdrop every day is forever, there is no going back to the beginning. These people here are for fucking real, certainly aint fucking tourists – 'That the new guy? Nuts, eh?' He hears the whispers – 'Wait tae ey sobers up!'

Still, he has his own corner in the ward. No one in their

right mind would wander into the cloud of flies, but there are few here of sound mind. Many natural wall climbers in one-man expeditions are caught on the wet sticky floor, and battered before they know what's happening, pockets turned over – mugged.

Big Haja pays daily homage; tablets, medicines, anything to survive – 'OH, MASTER.' He's seen them all. He knows the next designer jacket will be full-length plastic, with a zipper, the ultimate coat. Then life will get back to normal – 'Fucksake, eh. Always puttin es fuckin headcases oan oor ward, man,' he sighs, playing the double six – 'Am tellin ye. A know the score. S'a wind up innit. Fuck, chappin again.'

Big Haja knows, he knows something the others don't know, course he does. They all know something the others don't know, but the crash helmet in the corner? He knows nothing. He's long gone. The few brain cells left in his head have fried, been burned out before the natural rate of cellular extinction occurs – experience without memory.

AOOUUUWWW! AOOUUUWWW! AOOUUUWWW!

S'CUSE ME WHILE A KISS THIS GUY.

Chapter Eight

BARNEY FEELS REJUVENATED after a few days at home. The black eyes are turning yellow and the swelling is disappearing. He studies his face in the mirror – 'A wee bitta make-up, maybe even dye ma hair black tae. Aye, a disguise!' he decides, prowling through his mother's old make-up bag for the kit – 'Yes. That'll dae fur the mornin.'

Barney awakes in the morning. A cup of tea and scrambled egg on toast sit upon the mantle – 'Time is it, Maw?' he shouts.

Bessie opens the scullery door – 'Bernaard? Mer tea, son? The scullery's warmed up fur ye. Jist ironin a clean shurt fur ye. Ye cumin ben?' she shouts.

The heat from the gas oven hits him like a wave – 'Jesus Christ! Like an oven in here, Maw. Time wi ye up at?'

She stares at him – 'Aye, eh. S'gettin cauld, son. Supposed tae be summer. Eh? Wit? Am sayin it's SUPPOSED TAE BE SUMMER. Aye, eh. TERRIBLE, SO IT IS. Aye, terrible. S'NA LECTRIC FIRE A NEED.'

Barney sits down by the oven – 'Jesus,' he mutters – 'S'swelterin in here.'

He looks around. Shoes and clean socks sit under his chair. Their tartan pattern has huge white diamonds overlapping each other along their black band. He pulls them on. She has repaired the burst seam of the trousers too, with black thread – 'Al get in there fur a shave, Maw,' he says, pushing past her to the sink.

His eyes don't look too bloodshot he thinks. The dark glasses should conceal them and the make-up too would cover the yellowing bruises. He pats down his hair with a handful of Brylcreem. He keeps looking at it. The hair looks jet-black in the mirror but somehow it seems to turn navy-blue in the daylight, or is it just his imagination – 'Be swelterin the day again, Maw. Ma hair look awright?' he asks.

Bessie holds up the shirt for inspection – 'Aye. S'clean underwear there fur ye,' she says, pointing to the oven door – 'Leave they things an al wash thum. Yer hair? Aye, ye'v a smashin heid ey hair, son,' she smiles.

Barney turns his back to pull his trousers on – 'That's fine. How dae a look? Listen, is thur any auld jaikits here?' he asks.

She looks in the press amongst the pile of coats – 'This dae ye, son?' she asks.

He takes the full-length plastic raincoat – 'Aye. L'dae, hen,' he replies, grinning.

Bessie dabs at the sleeve with a damp cloth, leaving a huge dark patch – 'Wee marks oan the sleeve but ye canny notice,' she smiles – 'Aye eh. Ye look smashin, Bernard.'

Barney blushes, bowing his head boyishly – 'Aw turn it up, Maw. Godsakes, man,' he jokes – 'A plastic raincoat in summer?'

He pulls out a twenty-pound note. When she tries to refuse, he insists – 'Ma-ww. Noo take it, Maw. A mean it. Jist geez change fur the bus an you keep that fur messages.'

She has trouble staying on her feet. T-w-e-n-t-y-p-o-u-n-d-s? T-w-e-n-t-y-p-o-u-n-d-s?

She has to sit down for breath – 'Oh, Bernard! Twenty pounds? Fur me? Goodness!'

Barney throws an arm around her shoulder – 'Och. Don't be daft. S'only muney, Maw. S'only muney.' He breaks into a dance – 'An muney can't buy me lu-v! Can't buy me lu-uv! Can't buy me lu-uv!' he sings.

Bessie cackles – 'Yer an awful boay.'

He pockets the loose change – 'Right, then. Al probably be hame later. Don't wait up fur me. Aye, don't worry. Al watch masel. Naw, Maw, am noa in a gang. Godsakes, in a gang? Am sixty-odd! Right, cheerio. See ya later alligator! Da! ra! da! ra! da!'

She watches him dance out into the street – 'At the wi-ild croc-ad-ile! Sa-ee ya later! Alligator! A-at the wild croc-ad-ile! Da! ra! da! ra! da!' What an awful boy he was. A rascal, her boy, Bernard. He'd been all she had ever wanted – 'God luvs ye, son,' she whispers.

Barney adjusts the dark glasses and adopts a more sombre air as he walks along the street to the bus stop. No one will recognise him, he thinks. Brogan won't be all that difficult to find. He had a fair idea where to look but he did dread having to go into a poofs' pub. Brogan, he knew, was a good thief, but he couldn't understand why he'd become a degenerate, shagging young boys. He shakes his head. The very thought of having to go into one of these pubs to look for him fills him with disgust. He sees his reflection in the window of the bus shelter. No one will recognise him, he thinks, but then about a dozen kids descend upon him – 'Uncle Barney! Gonny geez two bob? Uncle Barney! Geez muney! Uncle Barney!' they're screaming.

Barney kicks their ball away, deflated – 'Fucksake! Beat it! Av nae muney!' he snarls.

The kids persist – 'Uncle Barney! Uncle Barney! Gonny geez

muney? Eh? Gonny eh, Uncle Barney? Gonny geez muney?' they screech.

He throws a coin a few yards away – 'Right, then! S'a scramble! Noo there! Ten bob! Noo goan! Beat it!' he sneers.

Some still tug at his coat – 'Uncle Barney! Gonny geez muney eh? Eh? Gonny geez? Uncle Barney! Eh? Gonny? Gonny geez muney fur sweeties? Eh?'

The bus is a relief – 'Right! Goan away fore ye aw get knoacked doon! Goan! Break intae a shop! Goan! Yer maw's goat sweeties fur ye! Aye, she wis lookin fur yes,' he sniggers, jumping onto the platform.

He finds a seat at the top of the bus. The conductor eyes up the sunglasses – 'Faresa pleasa,' he calls, walking up the passageway – 'Any faresa pleasa. Than-kupe!' Barney feels the finger prodding his shoulder – 'Oh, sorry, son. Eh, how much is it tae? Oh, dis this go near the West End?' he asks, staring beyond the conductor's shoulder.

The conductor points to the bus route maps that are plastered to the panels above all the windows – 'See that there, pal? That tells ye aw the routes. A jist cullect the . . . Eh? Wit wis that?' he asks.

Barney, lips trembling, barely audible, gulps – 'M'blind, son.' The conductor's looking at him suspiciously – 'Blind? How didye see the number ey the bus then?' he asks with narrowed eyes.

Barney turns away in disgust – 'Nevermind. There, take the fare,' he snaps – 'B'sellin fuckin raffle tickets next,' he mutters.

Harry Lauder's Bar, named after the famous music-hall entertainer of the Forties and Fifties, is situated on the corner of West

Nile Street and Sauchiehall Street. Barney pauses, pretending to be lost, before slipping through the doors. Satisfied that he hasn't been recognised by anyone on the street, he makes his way into the bar, safely assured that he hasn't been mistaken for a poof. He puts his sunglasses on the old mahogany bar, and in his deepest voice, orders a drink – 'Pinta heavy an a double, young yin.'

Barney marvels at the photographs set over and around the gantry. Barely an inch of space exists between the frames. It appears that every smile, every handshake ever made by the long-gone entertainer has been frozen indefinitely in black and white. A hushed atmosphere of reverence pervades the place; thick with the sleekit glances, and knowing smirks of people who live in the furtive world of homosexuality and fear.

Barney sups his pint, wiping the froth from his top lip with the back of his hand – Oh, a real man. Where's Brogan? he wonders. He orders another drink to kill the time, lest someone think that he was waiting for other reasons – 'Same again there, Jimmy!' he growls.

A tall gentleman in a navy-blue blazer, and cavalry twilled trousers looked at him from the end of the bar. The doll-like eyes and red nose were the hallmarks of an alcoholic. The Kelvinside accent reeked of whisky – 'Good efternoon,' he calls along the bar – 'S'terrible this hot weather, isn't it? Mind if join you?'

Barney nods – 'Aye'p. Roastin, eh?' he replies, trying to place the face – 'Naw, not at all,' he grins – 'Jist waitin fur a friend.'

The blazer joins him – 'Keptin George B. Tennent!' he declares, clicking his heels in salute an army officer styled – 'A drink?'

Barney liked toffs: they had money, education, money, culture, and money – 'Pleased tae meet ye, Barney Boone. Corporal, Highland Fusiliers, 1945,' he says, saluting the captain – 'Aye, a pinta heavy, thanks.'

George stands to attention – 'Bereny! It's a pleasure.'

Barney pulls out his bundle but the Captain is having none of it, the drinks are on him today – 'Bermin! Two doubles, thenk you,' he barks.

Barney stands to attention – 'A wee toast!' he swears, downing the double – 'Friends no longer wi us.'

George downs his drink too, bangs his glass on the bar – 'Yes, Bereny, to old friends.'

He sways a moment – 'Tell me Bereny. Where do you live? Do you still see old pels from the ermy then?' he asks – 'Never see eny myself.'

Barney looks misty eyed – 'Naw. Aw died, cept wan. Brogan. Chic Brogan. The two ey us wur in the trenches thegither,' he says hoarsly – 'Aye. Wee Brogan. Kerried um fur three miles.'

George is flabbergasted – 'Brogan? Smell, belding chep?' he cries – 'Bro-gan? Would you believe it. Bermin! Scotch! Two doubles, thenk you!'

Barney frowns – 'Dae ye know um then, Cap'n?' he asks.

George brushes flakes of dandruff from his shoulder – 'Know him? We're precticelly next door neighbours! Lives jest round the corner. Wonderful sense of humour. Chic, eh. Hmmm. Never mentioned the ermy. So he's your wee pel too?'

Barney looks off into the distance – 'Pels? Aye, we wur pels,' he grins.

Barney lurches down an imaginary memory lane – 'Aye.

Dark horse, the wee yin. Wis the same in the army. Never complained. Well, we wur fightin fur wur country!'

George couldn't agree more – 'Yes, yes, yes. Tough little bugger. Don't get thet sort enymore do you? Bereny! Tell me! Where do you live?' he asks.

Barney drains his glass – 'Maryhill, Cap'n. Been lookin efter ma muther since the war ended. Eighty-six she is. Faither left the poor wumin destitute. Ma army pension dis help, but well, ye canny complain, kin ye,' he says solemnly.

George signals the barman – 'Mervelous! Ebsolutely mervelous! Scotch please, end we'll hev two of your finest cigers, thenk you, sahhh!'

Barney can't believe his luck. He takes the cigar between his teeth – 'Thanks, Cap'n! Last time a hud wanney these, we wur in Flanders. Cheers, Cap'n. Yer a gentleman!'

George wards off his compliment, almost toppling over with the gesture. Barney has his eye on the possible descent of the man's wallet. Inside pocket, he thinks – 'Well, Bereny, don't think of it. Not often one gets the chence to meet en old scldier, eh. Oh bermin! Keep them coming please, thenk you, sahhh!' he orders.

Some eight whiskies later the Captain has begun swaying and slurring, rocking back and forth, signalling imminent collapse. Barney keeps his eye on that inside pocket. He'd be in and out of that pocket before the Captain hit the floor. He puts a steadying arm around the gentleman's shoulder, the arm of reassurance, but then just when the felling seems about to happen he feels the tap on the shoulder – 'Hallaw there, auld yin. Ye in disguise?' says a familiar voice.

Barney recognises the voice immediately – 'Aw, yer here ur ye. V'been here aw day.'

Brogan's bald head is gleaming as he nudges Barney – 'A see ye've met Big Spanky? Fuckin real yin, ye,' he sniggers.

Barney laughs – 'Spanky? Thought ey wis a Captain in the army?'

Brogan winks – 'Es awright. An alky. TV presenter. Aye, dis the news. Likes tae get spanked. Bitta rough. Anyway, wit ye daen in here? Ye lookin fur a boay?'

Barney looks at the two teenagers with Brogan – 'Nuthin yet. Here tae see you. Wee bitta business. Wantey get a seat? Who ur they two?' he asks, knowingly.

Brogan, dapper in his immaculately cut checkered suit, shirt and tie, acknowledges his two teenage escorts – 'Cuppla chickens. Ye interested? The wee blond geez ye some gobble. Kin huv a wee party later oan if ye want,' he leers.

Barney's horrified – 'Wit? Ye fuckin kiddin. Wit wid ma maw think? C'mon, leave the Captain wi thum tae we get a talk.' He turns to the two boys – 'Here, goan powder yer noses ur sumthin, hen, tae we get a wee blether.'

Brogan and Barney find a snug where they can talk privately – 'Wit the fuck's that you're wearin? Perfume?' Barney asks.

Brogan's tight jockey-build is reeking with cologne and aftershave, his head too has an extraordinary sheen. Barney persists – 'S'that furniture polish oan your heid?'

Brogan looks back – 'Furniture polish? You kin talk. Wit the fuck's that oan your heid then? Shoe polish? Yer hair's navy-fuckin-blue,' he sniggers.

He glances around, whispering out the side of his face – 'Right, en. Wit is it yer lookin fur?'

Barney slaps the bundle of notes on the table – 'Snout,' he says flatly, then touching his hair asks – 'S'dye. Kin ye notice it?'

Brogan ignores the question for the moment, as his eyes take on a gleam – 'Wee turn then?' he asks.

Barney smirks – 'Thur's a grand there. Am lookin fur snout. So ye in ur wit?' he asks.

Brogan rubs his hands together – 'Much ye lookin fur? S'it fags ur tabacaa yer efter?' he enquires.

Barney puts his hand over the bank notes – 'Any the two. Grand up front, so it's cut price. Am jist gettin an earner so don't geez any yer usual nonsense,' He signals the barman – 'Two doubles. Cap'n there's coverin thum. Well?' he asks.

Brogan's thinking, counting – 'Right, okay. A grand. Av goat snout, much as ye want. Fix a price in minute. Listen, a heard you're in bother wi that young team? Chibbed a burd up at the Woodside? That Jake. Barney, wit the fuck ur you daen graftin wi him? Am surprised at ye, auld yin. Thought you wur an earner. That wit the shoe polish an the make-up are fur? Ye in disguise?' he sniggers.

Barney turns chalk white – 'Yer kiddin, Brogan? Chibbed a burd? When wis this? Ad dun a turn wi thum but the coppers came oan tap. A goat oot oan a PF's release. Wit happened? The burd. Who chibbed ur?' he asks.

Brogan's grinning – 'Barney, Barney, Barney, wit the fuck huv ye dun? Ey thinks you grassed um.' He then asks innocently – 'Did ye? That urra boy Skud? He's been dun as well wi the bizzies. D'you get slung? Every cunt's talkin aboot ye,' he sniggers.

Barney blanches – 'Wit? Don't you fuckin start. Av never grassed an you fuckin know that, ya fuckin real yin.' He frowns – 'Jesus Christ. That fuckin boy. Fuckin headcase, so ey is. Chibbin a burd?' he murmurs into space.

Brogan digs the knife through the heart – 'Here, she's an

ex-copper,' he states matter-of-factly – 'Could be a heavy bowla porridge fur you, Barney!' He slaps a hand down on the table – 'Right. Al dae ye a wee favour, get ye oot the road tae the coppers nip that Jake. Wit ye goat, a grand?' he asks.

Barney's almost slumped in the corner of the seat. Jake, looking for him? Jesus. Get this snout punted and head for London. That's the best idea, he thinks. Jake won't be on the street long. A copper? A grass? – 'Right Brogan, much?' he asks dejectedly.

Brogan fixes his tie – 'A grand. Right, al gie ye a hunner-pun a snout. That's it flat, fur a grand, fair enough? That's hauf price. Wit you makin?' he asks.

Barney knows better than to tell him he's getting the full price from a fence – 'Aw, see you, ya miserable wee bastard. Always the fuckin same, so ye ur. A need a break an you're takin me tae the cleaners. Right, okay. That's fine then. Send wanney they wee poofs fur the snout. Al need tae get movin fore that young team try tae nip me. Right. A double fur me, c'mon, it's your round,' he says disgustedly.

Brogan pulls one of the boys over and after some whispering the boy disappears – 'Barney, c'mon noo. Nae need fur that kinna talk. Fucksake, am daen ye a favour man. Here, Auld Pop get a sixer? S'that right enough? Fur shopliftin? A sixer? Godsake man, es sixty-two. High Court fur shopliftin? Wit wis ey stealin? Gie um es due, graftin every fuckin day, man. Auld Pop, noo that man's an earner. Makes good muney tae.' He pauses for effect – 'Aye, Barney. Pop's a real grafter,' he smirks.

Barney knows the deal is done; time for a trip down memory lane, it's all we do these days, he thinks to himself – 'Aye, Chic, it's gettin harder,' he comments.

Brogan, the eternal optimist – 'Wit aboot this dope? It sells like fuck, canny get enuff ey it.'

Barney's brain is occupied with Jake. Jake – with a cleaver swinging in his direction. Chibbing a woman? Jesus. You didn't chib women. What the fuck is it all coming to, he wonders?

'Dope? Me sellin dope? Sellin dope it ma fuckin age? Nah, whisky dis me. But aye, a heard it sells. N'that urra swag aswell, H. Fuck that,' he says – 'Al stick tae earnin a wage, but it's gettin harder every day.'

Brogan nods – 'Aye, seriously, Barney. Guys ur aw startin tae get intae this dope thing. Aye, thuv goat this new mob called the drug squad. Heard they're settin guys up an ridin thur burds. Think it's gettin near retirin time, eh?'

He turns the conversation round to his favourite subject, the jail – 'See that Big Gypsy git murdured? Aye, fun um in a caravan, heid caved in. Wit ye gonny dae aboot this Jake? Oh here, by the way, who wis the darkie? Died doon the polis cells?' he asks, downing his whisky – 'Ye wantanurra? Lookin a bit white there, auld yin.'

Barney's brain is reeling. The Paki? That's why they slung him out. Now Jake thinks he's stuck him in. He holds his head in his hands. What a mess. They've killed a guy, and now they're lining him up to take the blame. The bastards, he thinks, they've set him up.

A blue blazer lurches over to the table – 'Cheps! Wit ye heving then? Wee Chic, eh. Never told me you kerried Bereny for twenty miles. You little bugger, ye,' he slurs, a slight breakdown in thet eccent becoming detectable – 'Two old pels eh. Bermin! My two pelshzz here would like . . .'

CLATERRRRRRRRRRRRRRRR!

Barney immediately picks him up off the floor, his hand a blur inside the blazer – 'Ohh, Cap'n! Ye awright there? C'mon, get a seat. Na-www. C'mon, time we got you a drink, for goodness sakes, man!' he declares.

Brogan looks at him with disgust – 'Coodny take ye anywhere, eh,' he sneers.

Barney chuckles – 'Wit? You spankin um ur somethin, ya fuckin wee real yin ye?'

Brogan shakes his head disapprovingly – 'Bloody disgrace.' Then whispers – 'Much?'

Barney looks at him while holding the captain upright – 'Much? Who you kiddin. Wit aboot aw yer shite a minute ago? Am daen ye a favour? Aye, fuck you. Here, c'mon there's yer wee boyfriend,' he sneers as the blond youth reappears – 'Right, here. A grand. Al leave the two holdall bags up at the George. Ye wantey charge me fur that as well?' he smirks.

Brogan bristles. He hates the poof label – 'Barney! C'mon noo. Much purridge'd wi dae thegither in Peterheid? Nae need fur that kinna talk. Here, d'ye mind the time a smashed up the roof? Jesus, the middla fuckin winter! Big McKenzie jist shouted it wis a fry-up fur the tea. Seven minutes a lasted! The shortest protest in the history ey Scotland.'

Barney sits staring at him as he takes off – 'A fuckin showin up. Comin back intae the hall! Kenny Kelly an Tony Smith! Aw laughin at me tae. A wis fuckin ragin. Ach, it's jist noa the same noo up there. That young team started attackin screws, fuckin pills, that wis the jail fucked. Cunts coodny dae thur time. Aye eh, Smith an Kelly. We had a laugh but this young team? Want ey be gangsters, coodny earn a penny eny thum. Wit aboot Raminsky? O'er the waw fore the screw finished the coont in the mornin. A liked auld Johnny. Goat oan really well wi

Johnny. That man had intelligence. Went behind enemy lines durin the war an widdae they dae – gie um a fuckin ten fur a safe! Gentle Johnny. Noo that's wit ye call a . . .'

Barney interrupts him – 'You a fuckin philosupher noo? Ya cunt, ye hud the best joabs in the jail. McKenzie's tea boy. Raminsky didnae even know ye.' He laughs – 'Nae cunt liked ye! Ach. Kenny Kelly eh. Ye don't get guys like that noo. Dae you mind when ey smashed the telly? Beat Gary Cooper tae the draw in *High Noon*. Right look, am off. Don't tell eny cunt ye'v seen me. This should get me doon tae London. By the way, am gettin the full whack fur the snout,' he laughs.

Brogan blanches – 'Ya dirty rat, ye. Aw well, thur'll be a next time, don't you worry. A hope that dummy's empty. Him? Big real yin, fuckin loaded. Al gie ye a smuther, but watch that young team, Bernard. Al see ye – pell!'

Barney salutes his old pal – 'Ebsolutely mervelous!'

They both roar with laughter as the bold Captain rouses to the sound of the Kelvinside River – 'Mervloush! Ebshlutely! Mervloush! Here! Bermin! Bermin! Where'sh thet bloody Scotch, shaaaah. Chic! You old derk horshe ye!'

Barney's relieved to have off-loaded the forgeries – and have the added bonus of thet bulging wallet in his tail. Wait till Brogan tipples, he thinks with glee. He hails the first passing taxi – 'Yoker, mate. Boclair street, son. Aye, 23. Naw, sorry it's 18. Forgot it's ma wee maw's am gaun tae. Swelterin, eh. Aye, hunner degrees.' he says.

The driver looks into the rear-view mirror – 'Aye, gets like an oven in here. Be gled tae get hame n get a wee bevvie. Knackered so am ur,' he replies.

Barney stuffs the now empty leather wallet down into the inside of the passenger seat and pockets the bundle of banknotes – 'Aye, jist got a good turn at the bookies there. Horse came up. Piggott again. Fifteen-hunner quid, less tax. Noa bad, eh? Jist gaun up tae square ma auld maw up wi a few quid. Murder, so she is. Sittin oot in the back aw day an en canny understaun how she's goat sunstroke? Oh, ye canny tell thum, kin ye? Ach, yer wee maw, eh. Where'd we be withoot thum, eh?' he laughs.

The driver laughs – 'Oh, ye don't need tae tell me. Goat ur an electric fire the urra day there. Know wit she's daen? Sittin wi that dummy coal oan! Aye, thinks it's real. The bills terrify thum, the poor auld cunts. Scared tae make a cuppa tea. A mean, they've wurked aw thur days an then wit – nuthin, some stupit pension, canny even feed thum never mind gie thum a heat. Aye, s'aw wrang. Then aw they bastards wi thur central heatin up in Barlinnie? Noa wit ad dae wi thum, the bastards.'

Barney shakes his head in disgust – 'Aye, a noa. Am gien ur a few quid the day then a need tae go doon tae London. Runnin a business doon there, antiques. Wantey make sure she's awright furst. Jesus, some traffic eh?' he comments.

The driver, smelling a huge tip turns the meter off – 'Al put it oan when we get movin. A don't like chargin passengers like yersel fur sittin in a traffic jam,' he winks.

Barney smiles – 'Good tae find sumbday wi a bitta integrity, son.'

The driver sighs – 'Ach, nae problem. A mean, where ur they aw gaun? S'always the same, innit? A like tae treat ma passengers fairly. Lottey these young drivers ur jist at it, if ye ask me. Busy the day eh.'

While they weave their way through the congested city centre another taxi has arrived at Boclair Street.

Bessie doesn't recognise the knock at the door – 'Wonder who that is?' she murmurs.

The figure at the door introduces himself simply as a friend of her boy – 'S'Barney in, Mrs Boone?' he asks politely.

Bessie's hand to her ear indicates her deafness – 'Tell ye the truth, am jist oot the day. Thought ad jist drap intae see how es daen, ye noa wit a mean,' he explains.

Bessie invites him in – 'Aw, son, ye'll be starvin then. Away ye go ben an huv a seat an al make ye a wee cuppa tea. Jamie, did ye say?' she asks.

Jake's just emerged from his third viewing of *One Flew Over* . . . – 'Fuckinhell missus. Ma name's . . . JAKE, HEN. J-A-K-E! Aye, that's it. Eh?' he explains.

Bessie smiles – 'There ye are, son. Jack? That's a nice name. Oh an look at they blue eyes. Bet ye'v aw the lassies chasin ye, eh? Bernard shoodny be long. Aye, an yer jist oot? These places, terrible eh? A don't know how they canny jist gie boys like yersel a chance. Aye.'

Jake's looking at her; nylons rolled around her shins, the floral apron, and slippers. A good ride would kill her, he thinks. S'no danger of him turning out like this, he silently vows – 'Eh, how's ey daen, enyway? Wit? Och, fur fuck sake,' he murmurs – 'A SAID, HOW IS EY DAEN, ENYWAY?' he shouts.

Bessie beams – 'Oh smashin, son. Gave me twenty pounds the day! Aye! Twenty! A nearly drapped when ey gave me it. Twenty pounds. Aye. Mer tea, son?' she asks.

Jake's eyes turn colder – 'Twenty quid? Noa bad, eh. NO BAD, ach fuck it,' he snaps, getting to his feet – 'Listen, al leave um a wee note tae get in touch. Jesus. A SAID AL LEAVE UM A WEE NOTE, OKAY?' he shouts.

Bessie nods – 'Aye fine, son. Mer tea? Oh a wee note, right then. Al get ye a wee bitta paper an a pencil, if a kin find wan. Es goat things aw o'er the hoos. Aye, an al tellum ye wur up tae see um, son. Sure ye don't want another cuppa tea? Ey shood be hame soon, ey said,' she explains. Jake digs the pencil into the piece of paper – 'Meet me the night in the George Hotel. Ye bettur be ther am warnin ye. Signed, J. P.S. Liked yer maw.'

He puts the open razer he's been palming back up his sleeve – 'N'thanks fur the cups a tea, missus. Eh? Aw, fur fucksake. A SAID THANKS FUR THE TEA, HEN!' he bawls.

Bessie lets him out – 'Fine, James. Nice meetin ye son, an you be good noo. Don't be gettin intae trouble wi they polis noo. Aye eh. Cheerio, son' she calls after him as he flits down the staircase and into the street.

Jake pays no attention to the taxi drawing up at the close. Stupid auld cow, he thinks. Should've ripped her. He ponders for a moment, but changes his mind. That fucking grass would drop dead if he had to walk into that, he laughs. Barney's mother sitting with her jaw torn open. That would have been a right laugh. Give Barney something to think about. The dirty grass, he thinks. Tied to a chair, face wide open, but no, this is for him, he decides, fondling the razor up his sleeve.

He walks along the street. Barney, he thinks. He'll get the message when he finds out that he's been up to his house. The note should make it clear that he means business this time. Poor Skud lying in that place. This is all his fault, he thinks. Barney, of all people. A grass. He can't believe it. After all the turns they had done together. The three of them working together and then this. He fingers the razor again. Bastard. It was out of order. Well, he was going to pay for it one way or the other. He had made his mind up on that – 'Fuckin chibbin this cunt,' he mutters.

The taxi driver can't believe the tip – 'A tanner! Ur you tryin tae be fuckin wide? Get oot this fuckin taxi fore a kick ye up the arse!' he shouts at the passenger.

Barney's looking at him, puzzled – 'Eh, witsat? Break ma jaw? Am a pensioner. Jist geez it back if yer noa happy,' he says, backing away from the driver's window – 'A don't know wit it's cummin tae these days. Ye gie a man a tip, an ey wants tae break yer jaw? Tae think av fought in the war. Sumthin wrang wi your heid, son.'

Bessie's at the window – 'Bernard! Bernard!'

Barney looks up – 'Be up the noo, Maw.'

The taxi blazes down the street to pick up another passenger – 'The George Hotel, pal, okay,' says the passenger.

The driver turns around in his seat – 'Don't pal me, son, okay. V'hud enuff pals fur wan day. Fuckin pals eh. Cunts,' he rants.

Jake flashes the razor in his face – 'Witsat? Wid you fuckin say there?' he demands.

The driver almost faints – 'Jesus! Naw look, mate! Am sorry! Honest! Av jist had this bastard there. Am sorry mate. George, son. Nae bother. Jesus,' he mumbles.

Jake leans back – 'N'turn that fuckin meter aff. Get wide wi me, ya prick.'

The driver stammers there's no problem – 'Aye, aye. Nae bother. Nae bother at aw.'

Auld Bessie opens the door – 'Mighta known. Missed that young fellah up tae see um tae. S'an awfa boy.' She takes his coat – 'Didye noa see um? That nice young boy? Jist missed um tae.'

Barney breezes past her, straight to her bedroom – 'Noa be a minut, Maw. Wit's that? A pal up fur me? Be oot in a minut,' he calls, stuffing the tobacco under her bed. He shoves the money inside a hole in the wall – 'Who'd ye say, Maw? James? James?'

The frown deepens – 'Wit ey look like? WIT? Long black hair?' he asks, panicking.

Bessie tries to remember – 'Aye, son, nice hair an blue eyes. James, ur wis it, am sure it wis James, ur wait a minut, wis it eh?'

Barney's legs are trembling – 'JAKE, MAW! WIS IT JAKE?' he shouts.

Bessie's face lights up – 'Jake! That wis it. A luvly lookin boay. Jist ootey jail. Oh, es left a note. Goodness, ma memory these days. Where'd a put it,' she mutters.

Barney's slumped in the chair – 'Jesus Christ, naw.' He's mumbling – 'Noa here. Noa ma maw.'

Bessie finds the note – 'Goodness sakes, there it is oan the mantlepiece. There it's, ye awright, son? Cuppa tea? Ye hungry? Al put some mince oan, noa be a minute,' she says, shuffling off to the scullery.

Barney's dumbstruck, mumbling – 'Jesus, wit um a gonny dae? Thuv set me up. That poor Paki tae. Thuv dun um in. Oh mammy daddy wit um a gonny dae? This bastard might chib ma maw noo if a don't turn up.'

He reads the note in desperation, eye's screwed up – 'Oh Holy Jesus. Wit am a gonny dae? This boy'll rip ma coupin wide open.' A panic twists in his belly like a tornado. Razors and steak knives flash before his eyes. Oh Jesus, no. His mother's face, with a meat cleaver smashing into the bone. This fucking psycho, he thinks. Jesus Christ. What's happening? He thinks he's been grassed. He would never do that. Fuck. He had never grassed anyone in his life. He's too old to take a chibbing. The cops? No. Never – 'Al never grass,' he vows.

Barney's face is ashen as his mother comes into the living room – 'Ther ye ur, son. Oh, son. Wit's the maitur? Lookit ye. Oh God, are ye awright?' she asks.

Barney waves her off – 'Naw, hen, am awright, honest, musta et somethin, at's aw,' he croaks – 'Pass in a minute,' he assures her.

Self-realisation sweeps through his bones; here is old age; those days of ducking and diving are truly over. Yesterday, the past, wherever it is, it is *now*. Then, in those days, he would have known what to do in this situation, but right now he feels battered, crippled, weary – immobilised somehow. A 'Why bother' feeling has taken tenancy of his soul. Christ, even the jail was a laugh, he thinks. He remembers his mates. They never bothered. Done their time, and got out. All those years, and for what? Where has it all gone? he wonders. All his old pals? Nearly all dead. God. He's just an old man – an old age pensioner. The image of himself in his head is devastating, decrepit, aged. He looks down. His hands. They look old. Old and battered. He touches his face, the pinkish-red skin mottled, blotched by a trillion tiny exploded veins; his hair, dry, lifeless, dead already – 'Whugh?'

Faces from the past smile at him – 'Noa long noo, auld yin!' they wink from nowhere.

Tony Smith's laugh pumps through his heart – 'S'Auld

Barney, eh. Face like a single end! Aye, eh. The lived-in look!' he'd said one time.

All his pals laughing, looking at him. They had loved him, these men – 'C'mon, ya'n auld cunt ye!' he hears them call – 'Wit ye scared ey?' they taunt.

Tony, eh. Nine stone, and ran Peterhead. AKA 'Skinny' if you were one of the boys. Not one screw said boo to him, he remembered. Tony, always a laugh. Four years he'd done for breach of the peace. Never a word out of him. Never complained. Done his time. Always carrying on as well, he recalled.

Christ. Who was it that said Hell was the Antarctic? he wondered. They'd said that the dead came back as penguins! That's right – 'Aye. Peterheid. Wit a place. Least we dun wur time when the jail *wis* the jail,' he sighs.

Wee Bennett, Auld Bullit Collins, Big Winning. All the right rascals. Standing out in a freezing wind. He laughs at the image of all those penguins, huddled together in one of those horizontal gales – 'Here, move o'er you. Staunin oan ma toe.'

Who are this young mob? The viciousness of this young boy – 'A like yer maw?' Who ever threatened the women? Men had it out in a back, or up the canal, man to man. Threatening your mother? Men didn't do these things. Men didn't chib women. Men were – men!

He pulls himself up – 'Aye, s'gettin dark, but noa jist yet,' he winks back to those faces from the past – 'Still a wee bitta life left in me yet fur this yin.'

He clenches his battered old hands into a ball, cracks the knuckles, and begins to feel the courage of youth again, coursing through his blood. C'mon, Barney. For fucksake, man. Pull yourself together, he thinks. Show this bampot what we were made of – a different breed. Real men – 'Hope ye'v kept a wee spot fur me, boys,' he whispers to his dead pals.

The trip through the valleys of nostalgia is shattered suddenly by a knock at the door. Bessie is pushed aside as a detective thrusts a search warrant into her face – 'Oot the fuckin road. Where's yer son?' he demands.

Barney appears at the living-room door as other uniformed policemen throw open the bedroom doors looking for him – 'Am here,' he says.

Barney knows that this is the retaliation for the bird in the Woodside Inn.

Jerry's in the lobby – 'Right then, turn the place right o'er, boys,' he orders.

Barney's rammed against a wall – 'Right! Where is ey?' the detective whispers in his ear.

Jake's note is crumpled amongst the embers in the fireplace – 'Where's who, son?' he replies.

Jerry batters Barney's head against the wall – 'Don't get fuckin wide. Am daen you wi enathin tae put you in Barlinnie. Know wit am gonny dae next? Put wurd in that your a grass. So where's the fly man wi the cleaver?' he repeats.

Barney's beyond intimidation – 'Fuck you,' he spits.

BANG! BANG! BANG! His head thumps into the plaster – 'S'at the best ye kin dae, ya fuckin haufwit, ye,' he sneers at the detective.

Poor Bessie begins wailing as she sees her boy; lumps of plaster and blood are stuck to his face like a grotesque mask

– 'Oh, Bernard! Bernard! Leave ma son alone! Holy Mother a Mary! Leave um alone, ya swines, yes,' she screams.

A policeman's voice calls from the old woman's bedroom – 'In here, think wuv goat a good wee result here, lads!' he shouts.

Jerry can barely contain himself as he sees the officer emerge with handfuls of packets of tobacco – 'YES! Right, you. Bernard Boone. I am charging you with . . .'

Barney interrupts – 'Here. Afore ye go any further. Name's oan that search warrant?' he asks.

Jerry looks at the warrant and back at him in astonishment – 'S'yer mother's address, but you live here,' he squeals.

Barney shakes his head – 'Told ye, son. Yer jist noa too clever at aw ur ye? Am jist the ludger here. Noa fixed abode as they say, eh, son,' he winks.

Jerry and the other policemen are staring at him – 'You'll let yer ain mother go tae the jail? Believe me, we're chargin ur wi housebreaking,' one says.

Barney closes the front door as they leave with his mother in handcuffs – 'If ma maw's breakin intae shops, son, that's hur business. Wit that wumin's daen in ur spare time's nuthin tae dae wi me.'

He slumps to the floor. What else can he do? he asks himself. Jake will terrorise her unless he makes the meet. There is no way out. This boy has no heart. S'a heartless bastard, he swears.

He picks himself up off the floor, staggering through to the scullery. He holds his face under the ice-cold water. Jesus Christ! Poor Bessie, he thinks. He never thought he would hear himself say it, but the coppers would look after her.

She was just an auld woman, never harmed a fly. They'll know the score. They know him, he would never let his own mother go to the nick. They'll tipple there's a move on – 'Right, en. S'time tae see this bampot. At least they never fun the muney.'

Auld Bessie, alone in a cell. The image of his mother alone, locked in a cell, spurs him on – 'Al show this fuckin haufwit,' he vows. Old instincts overwhelm his preparations for the confrontation – 'Magazines. A need magazines an string. Aye, eh. Al show iss bampot. The Auld Mob eh. String. Right, let's see.'

After punching holes through the mags, he laces them together with the string to form layers of protective padding. He looks in the mirror, tightening the body armour over his shoulders like a sandwich board – 'Stab me, eh? See aboot that. Need tae be up early in the moarnin fur me, son,' he grumbles, walking up and down.

He stares back in the mirror to see if the armour can be detected under his coat – 'Na. Canny notice it. Right, noo. Ma erms,' Two rolled up mags fit perfectly up the plastic sleeves – 'Okay, you guysh. You dirty rat. You hear? You dirty rat. Cagney, eh.'

He touches his face. Fifty years, he thinks. Fifty years graftin without a punch thrown and now this? At his age? He'd done time with real gangsters, real hard cases who could fight without blades – 'Blades? Mugs use blades. Noa a man. Naw, am gonny show this cunt. Big Collie Beattie never used blades. Hardest man in Glesga tae.'

Bang! Bang! Bang! He throws two left jabs, and a right uppercut – 'Wooof! Baaang! Jaw broke! How's thi . . . Bang! Bang! Bang!' He repeats the combination, over and over, until the timing's perfect – 'Oh, hullo there. Bang! Bang! Bang! Pick that cunt up!' he huffs and puffs.

He puts off all the lights in the house before finding his chair – 'S'better. Jist sit here fur a wee while. Gie um time tae get drunk. Al tobur this yin right up.'

God, Bessie, he thinks, staring into the fire – 'Hail Mary Fulla Grace . . .'

All he could do now was wait the few hours before heading into the city centre. Then who knows. He knew this boy would have a blade, but if he could just catch him with a few digs to the chin first – 'A grass? Al grass um the fuckin haufwit,' he says, looking at the clock on the mantle – 'Be shouting last orders shortly.'

Right. Time to make a move, he thinks. Take a taxi into the city centre. The George; he'll be in there. Should be drunk by now. He can see the bar in his mind. The place will be heaving as usual with all the thieves. The best thing would be to wait outside for him. Catch him off guard. He won't be expecting him to turn up. He looks around the house before leaving. He pokes the fire to make sure the coals are dead. He gets the money and puts it under the bed – 'Dae Bessie. Here wi go.'

Sanji waits at the desk after identifying his brother – 'Yes, sir, I'll be fine,' he tells the desk sergeant – 'I'll just take his things with me if that's alright?'

'S'fine wi me, son,' replies the sergeant without looking up – 'Somebody'll be in touch once the pathologist's report comes through. We think he may have been assaulted.'

Sanji feels an emptiness pushing through the doors to the station. God, how could it have happened? he asks himself. They don't seem to know anything – or they're not saying anything. His brother's face, the marks on his neck, how did they happen? he wonders. Have they beaten him up? Or was it other prisoners? They would just have to wait and find out.

As the temperature rose, the crack of a thunderclap erupted like a bullwhip above the city centre buildings. Lightning bolts followed, flashing through the streets just before the first few drops of rain lashed the pavement. Most people bolted for bus shelters, doorways, bars, anywhere to escape the sudden torrent of heavy downpour. All except one small figure in a plastic raincoat – 'Jesus. Never rains but it pours, eh. Summer fur ye, eh.'

Barney pulls back into the doorway of a pawnbroker's to avoid a soaking, but the coat is no protection. He feels the fabric gradually cling to his body like a used condom as the tiny splodges spread into a wrinkled layer of wet plastic – 'Hope these mags don't get soggy.' He looks above and across the traffic to the door of the bar – 'Should be last orders. Noa be long noo,' he mutters.

The butterflies in his stomach have begun to subside; the faces from the past help put fear aside, but the hollowness in the pit of his belly hosts deep terror. This is heavy duty, but he must go it alone – 'S'him ur ma wee maw.' Righteousness calls upon him to do the right thing. You don't let anyone threaten your mother. No, Jake has to be taken down. He's a bad element, a bampot, a shitebag – 'A like yer maw? Your gonny get hurtit, son.'

Cagney, eh. He steels his nerves with a grimace. James Cagney's face surfaces amid those from the past, strengthening his resolve to knock this boy clean out – BANG! S'a KO! Jake doesn't know it yet but he's in real trouble. Barney clenches a fist, punches the lump of knuckle into a flat calloused palm – 'S'ten noo. Right, Hectur.'

The George Hotel bar is heaving with punters. That old two bob on the bar is red hot. The elevated crowd holding up the bar are high on platform boots and lager while in the corner the heavy mob – beards and beads, leather and razors – sprawl the length of three tables, layered with pints of heavy, lager and cigarette stubs.

The last bell is ringing but no one's paying any attention to the clamour – 'TIME THEN GENTLEMENA! PLEASA! DRINKA UPA NOOA!'

Jake is hanging all over a wooden chair in the corner while the others create a huge circle around the altar of alcohol. The halfway hippies in Injun gear pass a reefer around below the cloud of smoke billowing overhead – 'S'good blaw, man.' Volcanic knees pushing up around the table have other ideas – 'Anurra lager?' And so it goes. Conversation evolves around stealing, blowing, fucking and football – 'S'Celtic playin away the morra? Magic. Dae a bitta graft afore the game.'

The shoplifters have had a prosperous day, they're selling three-piece suits – 'Tenner a whip. Aw the same size.' Pickpockets, too, flood the bar with gold chains, watches, rings, jewellery and kites – cheque books – 'Brulliant, man. Right in an oot.' Regular eight-to-five opportunists, chancers, try to put pint money together – 'Aw, c'mon man. Wee Dinky moturs. Nicker a go. Ye nae weans fur fucksakc?' they plead.

McGinty taps cowboy boots with his platformed feet – 'Jake. Ye cummin up tae wee Angie's? S'a party. Aw the boys ur gaun. Be a good laugh,' he smiles.

Jake's heels hit the floor as he swings forward to bang down an empty tumbler on the table – 'Angie's? A party, eh?' he slurs, puzzled – 'Fuck me. M'fuckin steamin here.'

He burps, lurching to his feet – 'See wit happens. The lounge oot yet?'

McGinty totters boldly to the door in a steady swagger – 'Catch ye oot er, Jake.'

The lounge is knicker territory, and couples only. You waited outside the lounge. You didn't go in. No, you hung around outside after the boozers, maybe nip a bird, maybe a party, maybe even batter some bampot for trying to pass through the drunken crowd on the pavement, but you didn't go in there. A lounge is for women. You drank in the bar with the boys.

McGinty leans back over the bonnet of a parked car. He's taking in the sights, scanning the flow of black mini-skirts, bulging blouses, tight jeans – 'Check they arses, man.'

He smiles as he sees Angie – 'How ye daen, doll? Wi gaun back up tae your pitch?'

Angie throws her arms around his neck – 'Johnny. D'you like me? Eh? Dae ye? Did Dawn say enahin aboot me?'

McGinty pulls her hips onto him – 'Dae a like ye? The fuck ye talkin aboot, man?' he croons into her ear – 'Ye noa a dae, doll. Here. S'at smell? D'you smell fish?'

Dawn looks over her shoulder – 'Here! Check hur!' she laughs, pushing her pals – 'Aw look at thum, eh.'

The small group of young women look over at the couple climbing all over the car bonnet – 'Get it oot, hen. S'it a big wan?' they giggle.

Angie's lost in feather-cut hair – 'Yer noa ridin me, by the way,' she mutters.

McGinty leans further back. He throws his head back,

laughing – 'Turn it up, man. Yer fuckin heavy. Honest, Angie, man, yer fuckin heavy, so ye ur. V'noa said a wurd, man.'

He's about to plunge her tonsils with his tongue when he catches a brief glimpse of a familiar silhouette approaching the crowd spilling out of the bar – 'That Auld Barney? Nah, canny be him.'

Jake's ulcer is playing up. He feels fire burning in his belly as alcohol scorches into a hole somewhere. He leans against the wall waiting for the bile to erupt when he sees two plastic shoes poking out of a plastic raincoat.

'Ye up at ma maw's, Jake?'

Jake's fingers curl around the razor in his pocket as he recognises the voice – 'How'd you get oot? Skud's in the bin, ya cunt.'

Barney takes a deep breath – 'Ye up at ma maw's, a said?'

Jake pivots himself against the wall – 'You're in fuckin trouble. F'you grassed yer gettin chibbed. Am tellin ye. F'a find oot,' he slurs.

Barney's heart's pounding, but he sneers – 'Listen. W'you up at ma fuckin maw's? Av asked ye three times. Ye fuckin deaf?' He leans into his face, hands behind his back for that quick combination – 'M'noa gonny ask ye again, son.'

McGinty sees them – 'The fucks he daen?'

Angie falls face first across the car bonnet as he brushes her aside – 'Johnny! Dae you . . . Oooof!'

Barney's feeling game. He goes to take the first swing of that combination, but what's happening? His arms are suddenly pinned to his sides – 'Wit the fuck?'

McGinty has him in a half nelson – 'The fuck ur you daen, stupit?'

Jake's hand snakes out – 'Fuckin graasss.'

The razor misses the target as his victim pushes back to avoid his jaw being torn open. The second swipe, however, connects, causing a tiny nick on the neck – 'FUCKIN GRASSSSS!' he snarls.

Barney doesn't feel anything, but the sudden gush of blood spouting from his neck is splashing all over him onto the pavement – 'JESUS!'

McGinty's face is hosed scarlet-red – 'Fuck!' he shouts, pulling his arms free – 'Fuck! Ma fuckin suit, man.'

Barney slaps his hand to the tiny wound, bursting the skin open even more. Blood is gushing from his neck. He feels his legs giving way as he clambers to hang on to the nearest lampost. He can hear women screeching – 'Arrrrggghhhhhh! Lookit that man's neck! Arrrrggghhhhhh!' The lampost light spins above him as he crumples up, and slides into the gutter, soaking in his own blood, the life force draining rapidly out into the night – 'Oh, God. A priest. Get me a priest, some cunt,' he gasps.

Jake stares down at him for a few seconds before staggering off down a lane – 'A told ye. Grasssss!' he shouts. He clatters into dustbins, skidding into the pile of stinking rubbish. He knows he's done the damage. That second blow. Fuck, he didn't mean to kill him – 'The fuckin prick!'

He emerges from the lane in a blind rage – 'A fuckin lifer,' he mutters to himself – 'A fuckin lifer fur that stupit bastard!'

He staggers blindly into people – 'Wit the fuck you lookin at?'

The thought of a life sentence is sobering – 'Here waita minut! Wis ey deid? Aw that blood, but maybe es okay?' he hopes.

*   *   *

Barney, though, lies in a pool of blood, staring forever up at the stars. Life leaks slowly from his body – 'A priest . . .' he whispers faintly, but no one is listening. They've shot the craw. You don't hang around when sirens are blaring louder and louder. You hit that sanctuary called an alibi – 'Been here aw night, boss. Barney who?'

The black uniform leaning over him offers comfort – 'Barney, ye awright, son? Dae ye know who dun this tae ye, pal?' he asks gently.

Poor Barney. He can barely whisper – 'A big ganga boays, boss,' he grins weakly. He feels the warmth of the copper's words – 'We'll get thum, son. You rest up noo, son. Al find these people.'

Barney gasps – 'Wit people? A fell, boss.' Those stars beyond the copper's shoulders burn brighter for few moments – 'S'that you, Bullit? S'that Wee Bennet wi ye? Where ur wi gaun? S'that . . . ?' His lips turn cold, an unmoving faint smile left behind for the world, the sentence eternally unfinished. The best thief in town has left for that other happy hunting ground where the pickings are ripe; the land where handbags are left wide open, the purses filled with money – 'Needin a haun there, missus?'

The copper puts a handkerchief over the dead eyes. He hears the ambulance siren as it screeches round the corner and on to the kerb. He waves them down, but they know already from the look on the copper's face – 'Sorry, lads. Gone. Poor auld cunt.'

A cauld wind blasts through the dark streets, howling fiercely and blowing mini-skirts across tight knickers, pimpling buttocks with icy specks of rain. People lean into the horizontal spray, protected by the beer.

Some are just too drunk to care – 'S'rainin! Haw, ha-aw!' Glesga, eh. Pure mental.

Barney fades to nothing more than a silhouette chalked on the pavement. That's how it is. Gone too are the punters. They bolted before he hit the ground, stampeding for the taxis, buses, lanes, anywhere not here. Rain disfigures the outline on the ground. There's nothing left, just that same old spiel – 'D'ye mind ey?' – 'D'ye mind ey, Auld Barney Boone?'

Barney who?

McGinty, Angie and Dawn sit huddled together at Angie's.

'Wit the fuck happened?' Dawn wants to know.

McGinty's stripped to his underpants in the scullery – 'Aw, fuck knows, man. That Jake cunt. Tanned that auld cunt right oot the blue. A thoat they'd jist . . .' He looks at the floor for a moment – 'Ach fuck, it's too late. S'that aw the blood aff me, hen? Any oan ma boady?' he asks, inspecting himself in the mirror – 'Imagine tae. That fuckin bampot. Pullin oot a razur? Barney tried to take a dig at um, but fur fucksake, man, thur wis nae need fur aw this.'

Angie rubs at a spot on his neck – 'Think that's it aw aff. Jesus. Johnny, wit ye gonny dae? The bizzies'll be lookin fur ye aw o'er the place. Wis ey really deid?'

Johnny grimaces – 'Nae borra, hen. Wit am a gonny dae? Nuthin. A wisnae there, so it's doon tae that bampot Jake. Sticks me in an al fuckin dae um in. Am noa daen a fuckin lifer fur that cunt. A fuckin razur eh, the prick.'

Dawn takes a drag from a joint – 'Jesus. Wit a kerry oan, eh. A think Jake'll be visitin Skud shortly. Wit wis it fur? Did the auld guy grass? Well, a think it wis a right liburty anyway. Slashin an auld man, fur fucksake. Fuckin ootey order so it is. Johnny. Wit wi you daen gettin involved anyway?'

McGinty shrugs those broad shoulders – 'Ach, fur fucksake, Dawn. Wit difference dis it make noo? S'long that cunt keeps ma name ootey this. A jist grabbed es erms cos a saw um gettin ready tae bang Jake. S'at fuckin drink, man. Geezat joint, fuckin heid's dun in, man.'

Dawn passes the joint – 'Right. Well, Johnny. We'll say ye wur wi us aw night. We'll say wi jist sat in the hoose. Say wi hud a party. Sumthin like that.'

Angie dries his back with a towel – 'Wit aboot yer suit, Johnny? S'covered in blood.'

Dawn takes the joint back – 'Skud's left gear in ma hoose. Al bring denims an at o'er in the mornin. Size a shoe ur ye? An eight? Hhmmmm. Thoat you'd a been a ten at least,' she laughs.

McGinty shakes his head wearily – 'Aw turn it up, eh. Fucksakes, man,' he grumbles.

Dawn throws her hair – 'Johnny! F-U-C-K-I-N cool it, man. Calm doon. Yer safe here. A said al get ye gear the morra. Jist huv a smoke an cool it, okay?'

Angie blindly pipes in – 'Aye. S'noa that, Dawn. Johnny wisny there . . .'

Dawn looks at her with narrowed, cynical eyes – 'Och, jist you shut it Angie,' she says quietly – 'Poor auld guy, coppin it fur nuthin.'

McGinty's nerves are getting the better of him – 'Aye, wanted a priest.' He takes a fit of the giggles – 'Probably've dipped es pockets!'

All three fall into hysteria, laughing uncontrollably – 'Aye, eh! A priest! S'cuse me father for I huv sinned!' McGinty does an impression of a priest – 'How long since your last confession, my son?' He's trying to keep a straight face – 'Eh, fifty years ago, Father,' he giggles – 'Auld Barney, eh? Aw fur fucksake, man!'

'Aye, eh! Barred fae heaven, eh! Stealin candles!' Angie squeals.

McGinty and Dawn are gripping their sides as tears stream down their faces – 'Jesus! Angie! Shut up, fur fucksake!'

Angie's loving it – 'Sentenced tae three Whole Marys! Nae time tae pay!'

Dawn's on the floor – 'Oh, Jesus. Angie, stop it ya nutcase!'

They pull themselves together – 'Oh, Jesus. S'that the hash?'

McGinty pulls on his trousers – 'C'mon, get a grip, man. Al wear these the night. New suit tae. Huv tae burn it the morra,' he decides. 'Bastard.'

Dawn agrees – 'Al take it away the morra an get rid ey the lot. Wit ye gonny dae? Ye better get a story straight fur the polis. People musta seen ye? Right. Al find oot the score furst, see if eny cunt's spoke tae the bizzies.'

McGinty begins to relax, rolling another joint – 'Right, Dawn. Jake. Where's he stay? Stull up in they auld hooses? Fucksake. Eh? Kin ey noa get a flat? Fuckin bampot.'

Dawn laughs – 'Him? Thinks es in the fuckin movies. Thinks es a cowboy. The fuckin haufwit. Noa goat that rolled yet?' she asks.

McGinty nods – 'Aye, fuckin bampot. Some gear this, eh. Paki black. Where did ye's get this?' he asks.

He then remembers the police cells – 'Here. Thur wis a Paki doon the cells. Barney an Jake rattled um fur a cuppla grand. Done a bogus oan um. Aye, Skud wis there aswell.'

Dawn sticks on some sounds – 'Wull noa play thum loud jist incase. Aye, Skud told us they'd done a turn, but said they wur fightin wi the polis, lost the money.'

McGinty frowns – 'S'at Otis Reddin? Brulliant, man. Fed up wi aw that Roxy Music an Bowie. Skud, eh. Wunder wit's happened tae that Paki? Barney goat oot. That wis how he goat eh, well.' The frown deepens – 'M'tellin ye. F'a get a pull fur this al tan that prick.'

Angie curls up at his knee – 'Es dead scared ey you, int ey, Johnny?' she asks, staring up into his face – 'You'd battur him, wint ye, Johnny?' she sighs.

Dawn smirks – 'Listen tae hur, eh.' She lies back on the floor – 'Johnny, geez that wee joint o'er here, roll anura wan anyway.' She sighs – 'Aye, eh. Wunder how ma man's daen in that place. That wis that bampot's fault aswell. Lettin Skud drap a tab? Then jist leaves um tae they bampots? That drug squad mob. Ey shood've handered Skud. He'd be oot the noo. The bastard, jist uses everybody, so ey dis.'

McGinty nods affirmation – 'Aye. The fuck did a get involved fur? Fuck. Barney wis ootey order, but.' He shakes his head – 'Stupit bastard so am ur. A saw Barney, but it jist looked like a daft argument, man. Know wit a mean?' he pleads.

Angie drops her head – 'Al visit ye, Johnny,' she whispers.

McGinty and Dawn look at her 'Visit um? Where? Och, Angie. R'you fuckin stoned? Goan lie doon fur fucksake, hen.' Dawn laughs – 'Am only kiddin, hen. Don't go in the huff, okay?'

Angie lifts her lovely head – 'Aye, am wrecked. But am jist

sayin. Eh, thingmy. Ehm. Wit wis a talkin aboot there?' she asks vacantly.

McGinty caresses her neck – 'S'awright, hen. A know wit ye mean.'

He builds joints one after the other – 'Wooof. Some gear, eh. Ye awright, hen?' he smiles.

Angie smiles pathetically – 'Aye, Johnny. Don't listen tae hur.'

Dawn rises up on her elbow – 'How? Wit've a said?' she asks.

Angie sits up – 'Naw, look. Am noa drappin hints ur anything like that. Dawn, your ma best mate. Know wit a mean. Honest. Am jist sayin, eh, thingmy. Eh, wit wis it again? Naw, right. Thingmy, that's it. Naw, wit am sayin is that eh, know wit a mean?' her wobbly head asks.

Dawn lies back down again – 'Johnny, keep thum rollin. S'gonny be a long night. Am a bit stoned masel. Makin tea, Angie?'

McGinty smiles; the hash melting those raw, jangling nerves – 'S'awright, Dawn. Good hash, eh. Wee Angie eh, bran new, hen,' he says reassuringly.

Angie melts before him, then, out of the blue – 'Right! That wis it. Ye kin stay here tae the bizzies urny lookin fur ye. Eh, Dawn?'

Dawn tries to climb up again, but is cut off before she can respond.

'Eh, Dawn? A mean. They won't look here, wull they? Right, but jist wan thing. Eh, ye canny, eh, thingmy. Know wit a mean?'

McGinty raises his eyebrows – 'Thingmy?'

Dawn sniggers – 'Aw, Jesus.'

McGinty is still confused for a moment before the penny drops – 'Aw, right. Thingmy. A seeeeee. That thingmy? That wit ye mean? That thingmy, eh?' he grins.

Angie squeals – 'Oh, Dawn! S'that noa terrible! Am stoned so am ur. Aye. Am noa a virgin ur that, but it's jist that, eh, well, ye canny, eh, noa the night. Right, who wants tea?' she asks, getting up – 'Noa be a minute. Two sugars, Johnny?'

McGinty and Dawn look at each other when she leaves. Dawn smiles – 'Ach. She's bran new, int she? Wrecked. That's aw. Did ye hear ur aboot the priest?' She leans over and whispers – 'Didny know wit we wur talkin aboot? Like that aw the time. Ach, a like Angie. Fancies you, Johnny. S'ur bad week. Aye, the thingmy.'

Angie reappears with tea – 'Yous talkin aboot me? Aye, right. S'he sayin, Dawn? Bet ye don't like ma tea,' she says, staggering around the coffee table – 'Ooops.'

McGinty sprawls over the easy chair – 'Magic, hen. M'fuckin wrecked. Ye goat a sper bed here, hen?' Angie resumes her position at his feet – 'Aye, ye kin sleep in mine the night. Dawn kin sleep in the urra room. S'at okay, Dawn?'

Dawn nods – 'Aye. Better noa hear yous two thingmyin, eh,' she giggles.

Angie squeals – 'Dawn! S'terrible! Av goat ma . . . Oh, fuck!'

McGinty's eyes are half-closed – 'Nae borra. S'better than that haunted hoose, eh.'

Angie looks puzzled – 'Haunted? Nae ghosts in ma hoose.'

McGinty sighs – 'Naw, Jake's hoose. They tenements. Ach, never mind.' He puts on another album – 'Marvin Gaye, man. Magic. Like Motown, Angie?' he asks.

Angie's blootered – 'Motown? Aw the records. Aye, Isley

Brothers. Huv ye heard that wan wi The Temptations? S'good, so it is. Otis Reddin's ma favourite.'

McGinty sees her in a new light – 'S'that right? Who else? V'ye heard *The Boardwalk*? Drifters? A luv that album. Aw this heavy rock shite's pure garbage. Fuckin longhairs. Drifters ur pure tops, man. Good fur shag . . . Eh. Oops.'

Dawn stirs from her stone – 'Am tellin ye, man. Yous two kin yap. Am shattured, so am ur. Think al go tae bed. Yous two gaun as well then?' she asks.

McGinty yawns – 'Aye, might as well.'

Angie gets up too – 'Aye. Am pure white. Am like a ghost, eh. S'noa haunted but, honest. Bet Jake frightens thum away, eh.'

Dawn reaches the door – 'Who?' she asks, confused.

Angie's hanging on to McGinty – 'Jake,' she grins.

Dawn frowns – 'Jake? Wit aboot um?'

Angie sighs – 'A bet ey frightens thum away.'

Dawn's puzzled – 'Who?' she asks.

Angie tries to keep a straight face – 'Jake.'

Dawn's befuddled – 'Wit aboot um?'

Angie laughs – 'Am jist sayin. A bet ey frightens thum away.'

Dawn's swaying around – 'Who?'

Angie's giggling – 'The ghosts.'

Dawn staggers through the door to the bedroom – 'Ghosts? Where?'

McGinty laughs – 'Jake's hoose, fur fucksake.'

Dawn looks at them – 'Jake's noa goat a hoose.'

Angie pulls McGinty – 'Och, c'mon.'

Dawn laughs – 'Aw, Jake's hoose? Right, a see. Ghosts.'

Part Two

'Make ma day, ya prick'

Chapter Nine

JAKE'S BURNING MORE doors in his derelict fireplace. Huge black shadows slither along the wall behind him. The rats, desperately careful to avoid attention, tiptoe along the skirting board. Their quiet has been disturbed – 'That fuckin grass!'

They observe the figure from a distance, from hideouts, holes, corners, concealed by the flickering darkness. Little black eyes barely blink; follow his every move. Instinct protects them from the bottle flying suddenly in their direction. They know that he is dangerous. They all are. Every one of them, killers. Alertness keeps them alive. The figure has been here a long time. He talks to the walls every night – 'Make ma day, ya prick.'

The cheap Vordo wine is scorching his veins, burning through his brain like a red-hot molten lava flow, boiling his blood with the firewater. He spits wine onto the flames. Whoosh! Burning wood explodes into a mass of sparks, the paint dripping into multi-coloured flares, lumps turning into smouldering embers near his feet. He ignores the tiny projectiles sizzling into his jacket. Fuck. He's a cowboy – man. He stares into the furnace, his face twisted with hate. A life sentence. Jesus. He couldn't face a fucking lifer. Ten years? Snecked and checked for ten years? The thought of doing ten years in prison penetrates his being, plunges through his black heart – 'Fuck.'

Murder – he always knew this would happen. He knew he would kill someone. There was always some bam out there looking for trouble. Some prick trying to be a fucking wido. Did he look for bother? Kept to himself, didn't he? Aye. Some fucking bampot, trying to be wide. Another innocent fucking victim in the court – 'An then grassin ye.'

It was in his blood to kill. But not like this. A wee nick on the neck? This was stupid. There wasn't that final blow, like a real murder. He felt no satisfaction. No high. The physical release from a fight. No; he felt cheated. Killing an old man? He should've been high, a winner – 'Fuckin grass, anyway.'

Dawn and Angie. Where did they go? They would be worrying about him. McGinty too. He'd been right in. Probably knew that auld bastard had a blade. Aye, eh. They want to be fucking widos. Imagine? Coming down to the George? To look for him? Nah. He'd a blade on him, definitely. McGinty must have seen something. He knew right away. Fuck. Skud will be killing himself laughing now. Wait and see. Soon as he hears about it, he'll know – 'Aye. Jake done that fuckin grass fur me.'

Jake slugs more wine from the bottle – 'Fuckin bizzies,' he laughs – 'Be lookin fur me noo aw o'er the place. That fuckin auld grass.'

News bulletins flash before his bloodshot eyes – 'Murder Hunt. Suspect is armed and dangerous. Police warn public not to approach this man. He is extremely dangerous. He is not to be approached by any members of the public.'

Aye, he thinks – 'Armed an Danjerus. That's me. Furst cunt that comes near me's in trouble. Es gettin it. Noa takin me alive. M'tellin ye. Al get a shotgun. A sawn-aff.'

He spits more wine into the fire. Whooooosh! Aye. A shotgun. Show these bastards. A lifer? – 'Aye. S'a fuckin sawn-aff am gettin.' Armed and Dangerous? Trouble? Not to be approached? Aye. He'll show them trouble, real fucking trouble.

'Ye's wantey go ahead, ya cunts?' he shouts – 'Eh? Want fuckin trouble? BANG!' Aye. He'll give them trouble alright – 'BANG! Eh? Fuckin bampots. McGurk's the fuckin name. Jake McGurk, ya cunts,' he roars, spinning around with that invisible shotgun – 'BANG!'

A huge rat is caught off-guard. Should have been watching. The empty wine bottle smashes into its side, breaking its back legs on impact before exploding all over the floor. He lurches over. The rat's squealing, but the sound is stamped out by the heel of a cowboy boot crunching its head into the floorboards.

'Fuckin longtails. Noa be eatin anymer fuckin cheese, wull ye!' he laughs – 'Hickory fuckin dock, eh.'

Jake bursts open the carry-out bag – 'Auld cider eh. Mind when a wis a boy. Doon in the dunnies.'

The image of an empty dungeon flashes through his brain – a dungeon waiting for his presence. A lifer. His stomach seizes up with the thought. A dungeon for life. Fuck. He can't face it. Be better to just get it over with. Go out in a blaze with the coppers. Aye. A shotgun. Double-barrel. Fuck it. Who the fuck wants to grow old anyway? Fuckin coffin dodgers. Difference does it make? Today. Tomorrow. It's all the fucking same. Later: now. You go anyway. Fuck it. Ain't no going back now. Naw. Fuck it. He's going ahead. There's nothing to lose. His life? What life? Five minutes we're here. Five fucking minutes – 'Loada fuckin shite,' he slurs.

He slouches into a corner, watching the flames. Never see a fire again. Never walk in the rain. Never fuck a woman. That's what life means. That's what jail is. Some daft screw telling you when you can piss, when you can shit and sleep. No, no, no. That's not for him. Freedom means everything. He can do whatever he wants out here. He can. Well, he can piss when he feels like it. A lifer, eh – 'Nae fuckin chance.'

There's nothing like murder to wake you up to freedom. Friday nights by the fire, kids and the wife, these things don't seem so bad after all. That boring life. Surely it's better than some dirty hole in a jail. That's murder for you, some dark fucking hole.

He feels the flames burning his face. He stares into them. Aye. A shotgun. He sees a police cordon. They're waiting for him – 'C'mon, ya fuckers.' Aye. Daft coppers. The pricks won't know what's hit them – 'BANG! BANG! BANG!'

He's running at them, shotguns in either hand. Aye eh. Panicked, the cunts. Fucking shitebags. They're looking for him? See about that. He's looking for them. Shotgun in the face. See who's looking for who. The cunts – 'MCGURK'S MA FUCKIN NAME!' he roars – 'JAKE MA-FUCKIN-GURK!'

Dawn, he thinks. Need a talk. Visit Skud. Then that's it. Go ahead. Skud – 'Ma best fuckin mate.' Barney should never have grassed. He liked him, but you never grass a guy. The stupid bastard. He should never have come looking for him. Things would have worked out. Why did he have to come down to the George? Fucksake. He put everybody in a bad position. He would have gave him a mouthful, maybe a punch on the jaw. Stupid bastard. The George? Must have had a message on him. McGinty definitely tippled. Imagine? Anyway, too late – 'Fuck it. M'fuckin gaun ahead.'

McGinty opens his eyes; daylight filters through a narrow gap in the curtains. Angie lies beside him, curled up into a tiny ball.

The previous night's events hit him. Did it really happen? he wonders. Why haven't the police chapped the door? They'd have done the rounds, surely. Maybe Barney isn't dead. Maybe Barney was at it? Playing possum? He'd do that. He can't be dead. We'd have heard something, surely? He hadn't done anything anyway. All he did was grab his arms. Fucksake. He'd tried to stop the fight so what was he worrying about? Anyway, Jake'd done the business, not him. Nah. He must have been at it. That blood. Was it as bad as it looked? That might have been the drink. Things look worse with the drink. Nah. He can't be dead. They would definitely have heard by now – 'Fuckin auld real yin,' he laughs.

Angie stirs – 'Who's that?' she asks.

McGinty turns over – 'S'me. Who did ye think it wis?'

She relaxes again – 'S'at you, Johnny? Fuck. Didny know where a wis there.'

McGinty lights the half joint lying in the ashtray – 'Wanta draw?' he asks.

Angie says no – 'Too early fur me. Time is it anyway?'

McGinty doesn't know – 'S'early. Listen. Barney might noa be deid at aw. D'you remember anythin fae last night, hen?'

Angie turns her back to him – 'Last night? Wit ye talkin aboot?' she mumbles – 'Ach, am gaun back tae sleep. Ye noa tired?'

McGinty feels better. Angie would have remembered. It couldn't have been that bad. Did Jake get him on the neck? Might have been his ear. They bleed like fuck. That's what's happened. The blood's been from his ear. Fuck. All that worrying. The hash just makes it all seem worse. Blows it out of proportion. Wait and see. He'll swagger into the George. Aye. Guaranteed. That's what's happened. Auld Barney, eh.

Never misses a trick – 'Fucksake,' he laughs – 'Ma fuckin suit ruined tae. Wait tae a see the auld cunt.'

He takes a long deep drag – 'Fuckin auld bam. George'll be mobbed the night. Catch um in there,' he decides.

Angie's bum is pushed into his thigh – 'Jesus,' he sighs, feeling his prick – 'Angie, ye sleepin?' he whispers, rolling onto his side – 'Angie?'

Angie feels the prick slide into her, but doesn't resist – 'Hhhmmm. Wit ye daen?' she whimpers – 'Stop it. V'goat ma dabs. Oh. Johnny. Stop it. O-oh.'

McGinty groans as she begins to push back.

'Stop it, Johnny. Ma dabs. Ye'll get aw blood. O-oooh.'

McGinty starts to slip and slide – 'Ugh, ugh, ugh. Fuckinhell, man. Aw, Angie ba-aby. Oof, oof, oof. Geez yer arse up. C'mon. Up oan yer knees. That's it. Aw, aw, aw-w. That's it. Right up. C'mon noo. Ye-es. Ugh, ugh, ugh,' he grunts.

Angie's legs are spread, her arse exposed – 'O-of. Oh. Joh-nny. O-of, oof, oof. Stop. Oh. Joh-nny. Stop it. O-of. Je-sus. O-of, oof, oof.' She feels his hands gripping her thighs, his finger pushing into her arsehole – 'Johnny! Naw. Noa there. Naw. Sto-op, please. Don't. A don't like that.'

McGinty's face glares down at her back – 'Shut the fuck up, ya cow. Ugh, ugh, ugh. Oooyafucker ye. Shut it. Get yer arse up. Ugh, ugh, ugh. Shut it. Am cummin. Urgh, urgh, urgh urg-hhhh, ya fucker ye,' he growls as the both of them collapse onto the mattress – 'Jesus. Aw Angie, fuckinhell, man. Aw fuck. Ma-annn.'

McGinty lights up a cigarette – 'Ye awright, hen? Wanta a fag?' he asks.

Angie rolls onto her side, cuddling him – 'Aye, geez wan. Jesus. That wis sore, you,' she laughs.

McGinty grins – 'Think a wis gonny dae yer arse?'

Angie punches him – 'Aye. That'll be right, you,' she says sarcastically – 'A don't like daen that.'

McGinty leans up on his elbow – 'How. Ye dun it afore?'

She punches him again – 'Aye, right!'

Dawn hears the laughing from the other room – 'TURN IT UP!' she calls – 'Angie. The time. S'the time?'

Angie shouts back – 'S'early. R'ye cummin ben? V'gotta a joint.'

Dawn's pulling the quilt around herself – 'Paira real yins. D'ye never stop yappin?'

Angie beams at her – 'R'ye makin tea? Aw c'mon. A made it aw night. Awch, Dawn. Goan eh. Ma mouth's bone dry.'

Dawn gives her a look – 'Al bet it is, eh,' she quips. She passes back the joint – 'Right, a suppose al huv tae. Two sugars, Johnny?'

McGinty's propped up when she returns – 'Here. A don't think es deid, ye know,' he says – 'We'd a heard somethin, wint wi?'

Dawn lights a cigarette – 'Who, Barney? Am noa sure. Wit aboot aw that blood?'

McGinty dismisses her point – 'Cooda been the ear. Mighta been es ear. They bleed like fuck.'

Dawn ponders a moment – 'S'right enuff a suppose. The bizzies wur there. Aye, we saw thum.'

McGinty laughs – 'Och, fur fucksake. They're always hingin aboot the George. Fuck. Barney's an auld wido, ye know. Am tellin ye. Yous don't know um. Wide as fuck, so ey is.' He looks out the window – 'Nah. The bevvie and the hash. We wur aw blootered, an mind we aw bolted. Every cunt scattered, dint they? Nah. Am gaun doon the toon the night. Fuck. Wur aw panickin fur fuck all,' he declares.

Dawn shrugs her shoulders – 'Ach, fuck knows. Suppose yer right. Anyway. Wull you stop playin wi his baws under the blankets?'

Angie squeals – 'Wit? Dawn!'

Dawn is shaking with laughter – 'A kin see yer haun!' she screams – 'Jugglin away there!'

McGinty laughs – 'C'mon, wull get up anyway. Dae a coupla joints.' He throws a leg over the side of the bed – 'Aw that worryin, fur fuck all. Fucked ma heid up last night. Here, did ye clock that Jake? Staunin at the door last night? Definitely thinks es in a cowboy movie. The man wi nae name eh!'

He chuckles – 'Ach, Jake's okay. S'noa bad cunt. Hander ye if ye wur in bother. Aye, es a game cunt. Don't be kidded, Dawn.'

Dawn snorts – 'Hander ye? Didny hander fuckin Skud. Nah, Johnny. Guy's a wanker. A canny stand um. Pure fuckin trouble so ey is.' She then turns to the bundle in the bed – 'Right, c'mon you. Up!' she laughs, pulling back the bed cover – 'C'mon! Up!'

Angie squeals as the blankets are pulled back – 'Dawn! V'nae knickers oan!'

McGinty hits the living room – 'S'thur any grub, Dawn? M'fuckin starvin so am ur.'

Dawn sits down on the couch – 'Think thurs beans. Beans n toast dae ye the noo? A canny cook. Angie canny cook either. Nae luck, eh,' she giggles.

McGinty begins rolling – 'Great.' He brushes the album cover clean to roll the joints but does a double take – 'Dawn. Check. Mantavani? Fuckin nuts int she?' he laughs.

Angie appears in a quilt – 'Yous talkin aboot me?' She takes the first joint – 'Freezin innit. Supposed tae be summer tae.'

Dawn turns to her – 'Find yer knickers en?' she smirks – 'Cuppa tea there fur ye. Wull a stick the fire oan?'

McGinty leans back – 'Wooof. Some fuckin blaw that, eh. Wit yous daen the night en? Ye's gaun doon the toon?'

Dawn can't be bothered – 'Ach. Fed up wi that George. Might jist stay in. *Starsky an Hutch* ur oan later the night. Might jist stay in an watch that ur *Kojak*. Wull see.'

Angie squeals – 'Ur they oan the night? Aw brulliant. Ye stayin here, Dawn? Wuv got plenty a blaw. Al go fur sweeties later oan.' She claps her hands – 'Brulliant. A like Starsky.'

McGinty smirks – 'Paira fuckin bams. Listen, eh. S'it awright if a come back the night, Angie?'

Dawn throws her hair back – 'S'awright if a come back the night, Angie?' she mimics.

Angie looks at her – 'Witsat? Wit's the matter wi ye? A never even said anythin!' she protests.

Dawn takes a long drag – 'S'noa you am oan aboot,' she says, exhaling.

McGinty raises his hands in an appeal – 'The fuck did a say?'

Dawn shakes her head – 'Disnae matter.'

Angie knows what's wrong. Dawn's missing her man – 'R'ye missin Skud?'

Dawn nods – 'S'that bastard. Swaggerin aboot, an ers Skud. Fuckin binned up. Ach. Am sorry, Johnny. S'noa your fault. A jist hate that guy.'

McGinty tries to cheer her up – 'Be brand new, hen. Skud'll handle that fuckin pitch. S'fulla fuckin bampots. Skud'll be takin pratection muney. Ye know wit es like.'

Dawn looks away — 'Am jist pissed aff. C'mon you. Beans an toast fur Johnny. Guys fuckin starvin so ey is,' she says suddenly.

Angie throws her hands up in protest — 'Dawn! A canny cook!' she squeals.

McGinty dances around the scullery — 'Where's the stuff?' he shouts — 'Aw here! Yer fuckin kiddin! Thurs eggs an aw that here! Al make a breakfast, okay?'

Angie floats through to help — 'Wanta haun, Johnny? Listen,' she whispers, 'Dawn's awright. Jist missin Skud. Ye cummin back the night?'

McGinty looks at her — 'Aye. Might as well, eh. S'it okay?'

Angie beams — 'Aye, Johnny. Aye, honest. Dawn'll feel better wance she's hud a coupla joints. Dae you like me, Johnny?'

McGinty looks at her again — 'Fuck me, man. You never stop dae ye?'

Angie squeals — 'Naw. Johnny. A didnae mean it that way. Honest. Am jist sayin ehm, eh. Fuck, am stoned already.'

McGinty cuddles her — 'Ach, yer bran new, hen. Here, butter the breed. Here. Listen. Dae ye like The Moody Blues? Good oan acid. Aye, av goat aw thur albums. Bring a couple up fur ye.'

Angie turns all shy — 'Thanks, Johnny. Ye kin stay here if ye wanty. A meant wit a said last night.'

McGinty gets the plates — 'Eh? Ye talkin aboot? Last night?'

Angie bows her head — 'Al visit ye.'

Dawn looks round the door — 'Aw, fur fucksake. Canny leave yous two fur a minute. A hope you washed yer hauns?'

Angie squeals – 'Dawn! S'terrible! A wisnae playin wi es thingmys.'

McGinty wolfs down the breakfast – 'Fuckin starvin er so a wis,' he says, lighting up another joint – 'S'that fuckin hash, man. Starvin aw the fuckin time.' He takes a drag down into his lungs – 'Fuckinhell, man. Listen, kin a get a wash? Dawn. Ye gaun o'er fur that gear? The denims an at? They Levi's, by the way?' he asks.

Dawn passes the joint – 'Aye. A furgoat aboot that. N'fact, al get a taxi the noo. Noa take me five minutes. M'gettin stoned masel. Need fags ur anathin? Right. Noa take five minutes,' she says, getting up.

Angie jumps up – 'Wull a go way ye, Dawn?' she asks, but there's no need.

'Don't be daft. Al noa be long,' says Dawn.

McGinty flops back on the easy chair – 'Thanks, Dawn. Al get a wash in a minut. Dae a joint fur ye cummin back, okay.'

Dawn smiles – 'Check hur.'

McGinty looks – 'Ach. Bran new, int she?'

Angie looks up from the floor – 'Wit? Yous talkin aboot me there? Wit? Wit yous sayin? C'mon, noo. That's noa fair.'

McGinty plonks himself down on the chair next to her – 'Stick oan Otis Reddin.'

Dawn shouts from the door – 'Johnny. Watch yersel wi that yin.'

Angie squeels – 'Dawn! S'terrible!'

McGinty fingers her hair – 'Ach, yer awright, hen. Windin ye up.'

Angie looks up at him – 'A know! Ach, she's ma pal. A tell hur every-hing. Went tae school thegither so we did. A kin tell ur anathin. Missin Skud, so she is. Skud's a laugh aswell. S'Jake scared ey you, Johnny?'

McGinty slides down the chair, stoned – 'Jake? Wit aboot um?' he asks.

Angie leans on his knees – 'Am sayin is ey scared ey you? Jake.'

McGinty shrugs – 'Jake? Jake's okay. Wur mates. Skud tae. We aw went tae school thegither.'

Angie fingers a circle on his knee – 'Aye. We wur at school thegither as well. Dawn an me. Dae you like me, Johnny? Naw, dae ye? Ye don't huv tae say anathin. Am jist sayin ehm, eh. Know wit a mean? A meant wit a said last night. Am ded serious an at.'

Dawn returns twenty minutes later with a plastic bag – 'Denims, shurts. Try thum oan. Skud's the same size as you. They shood fit nae bother,' she says, puffing – 'Where's the joint. Right, hen, hanks.'

Angie takes the shirts out – 'Aw, Dawn. Skud's denim shurt. Kin a wear that? Thanks, pal. Johnny?' she asks – 'Wull you wear it the noo an al thingmy it later. S'that okay, Dawn?'

Dawn shakes her head – 'Jesus Christ.'

McGinty tries the shirt on – 'S'that fit? Av got broader shooders than Skud. S'it look okay?' he asks them.

Angie fixes the collar – 'Aye. Ye look like eh, wit's es name, eh thingmy. Dawn. Wit's his name that wears the denim shurts oan the telly? Och. That guy. Aw, wit's es name again. Johnny, dae you know who a mean?'

McGinty frowns – 'Oh, aye. Him. Black hair? Big guy?' he teases.

Angie squeals – 'Aye, that's him! Black hair! Right! An es big! S'es name again?'

Dawn sighs – 'Angie, lie doon, hen. Jesus Christ, man.'

Angie's deflated – 'Eh? Wit? A wis jist sayin.'

McGinty hands her the joint – 'Know who ye mean,' he says, heading for the kitchen to have a wash, and then getting into in the new gear – 'Noa bad, eh?' he asks them.

Dawn looks up – 'Aye. Ye look luvely.'

Angie's eyes light up – 'Wow! Ye look like a thingmy, a guy cuttin trees doon. Dawn. Dint ey?'

Dawn rolls her eyes – 'Ye rollin a joint?'

McGinty builds the skins up – 'Cuppla joints an am off.'

Angie decides to make tea – 'Oooops,' she giggles – 'Tea, Dawn?'

Dawn apologises – 'Aye. Listen. Sorry am bein heavy. A don't mean anathin. Av jist got a lot oan ma mind the noo.'

McGinty looks up from the skins – 'Ye don't need tae apologise,' he smiles.

Dawn looks at him blandly – 'Apologise? A wisnae talkin tae you, Hector.' She turns to take the joint – 'Nah. M'only kiddin, Johnny. Hud ye gaun there, eh?'

Angie sigh's – 'Aw, Dawn. Am yer best pal. Fuck. A thought ye'd fell oot wi me er. Ye awright noo?'

Dawn cuddles her – 'Och, don't be daft, hen. Am jist stoned. Thinkin too much. Right. C'mon, get the telly oan. Cartoons ur oan. Who's turn is it fur the tea? C'mon noo!'

Angie squeals – 'Brulliant! Thurs a film oan later tae. Wull jist stay in. Get stoned thegither.' She turns to McGinty – 'Ye cummin back, Johnny?' she asks.

McGinty looks out the window – 'Turned oot noa bad, eh? Aye. Al be back later. Am jist huvin a cuppla pints the night.

Fuckin steamin the noo, man. Right. Listen. Dawn, al whistle up, okay, so ye know it's me. Don't need a kerry oot dae wi? Nah, the blaw's anuff innit. Right, am off. Al see ye's later oan, okay.'

Dawn smiles – 'Right, Johnny. See ye later. See if thurs any young guys oot there. Av goat the horn here!' she giggles.

Angie squeals – 'Dawn! S'terrible!' She kisses him at the door – 'Right, then. See ye the night, eh.'

Dawn laughs as she hears her whisper to him – 'Dae ye like me? Ye don' huv tae say anathin the noo.' Poor Angie, she thinks – 'Wit a shame.'

McGinty slaps her arse – 'C'mon, you. Yer fuckin heavy, man. Ehm. Listen. V'ye any muney?' he mumbles.

Angie squals – 'Aye. Much dae ye want? See! Knew ye liked me aw the time.'

McGinty tongues her at the front door – 'Thanks, doll. See ye later, okay.'

Dawn and Angie curl up together on the couch – 'Shut they curtains, Angie. Cartoons in a minut. Johnny's awright.'

Angie giggles – 'Ey likes me. Asked me fura tenner.'

They finish a joint and stare at the television screen – 'Angie, roll a joint an al make us a cuppa tea.'

Angie builds the skins – 'Brulliant, cartoons n a movie. Don't let me faw asleep, Dawn. Ye know wit am like wi movies.'

Dawn smiles – 'Jesus. Disny know wit day it is.'

Chapter Ten

JAKE TRIES TO squeeze his eyes closed again, but that dazzling bright daylight flooding through the tenement is penetrating the lids. Everything is red behind them. He rubs them, blinks a few times, and lights a cigarette. Fuck, he thinks. Have to pack in this smoking lark. He coughs up. The spittal lands on the opposite wall. He takes a drag to ease the tight steel band gripping his dried brain. Fucking drink. He sees the two empty wine bottles. The third is missing. What time is it? he wonders. What fucking day is it? He gets up to take a piss in the corner. He kicks the dead rat away – 'Fuck did that thing come fae?'

He leans his head against a wall to piss down a hole in the floor. He looks down the hole. He then looks at his feet. Blood? – 'Fuck did that come fae?'

FUCK. Last night. FUCK.

His dick shrinks in his bloody hand. FUCK. Barney. FUCK.

His legs almost give way. FUCK. He spews up all over his feet.

M-U-R-D-E-R. FUCK. FUCK – 'Aw, fur fucksake, naw.'

He tries to piece it together. Barney saying something to him – getting wide. He grabs for his pocket. The razor? A weapon can link him to the murder. That's all they need and he's done. He clutches the black lacquered handle – 'Thank fuck. Get rid ey this later.'

He hunches down in the corner to think. All that blood?

The blade must have hit the jugular. Fuck. Why the fuck did he have to get wide? Too late now. Life. Jesus, he thinks. There's no way he's going to the jail. This is it. Crunch time. Well, he thinks. It was going to happen anyway. One way or the other. Some cunt was going to walk into it.

He a takes deep breath – 'Get some bombers later. Fuck it. Wers that cider?'

He gargles the first mouthful and spits it all over the floor. Fucking pish. He swallows the next slug. Gulps it down to clear his head. A lifer. Jesus. This is definitely it. A lifer would destroy him. Might as well end it out here. There would be no point to the jail. He'd seen too many pals get lifers. Never hear of them again, he recalls. Nah, he can't see the point – 'Fucksake, Barney.'

He pulls himself together. Right, he thinks, a plan. Get a shotgun. Lie low and wait a few days. Take it from there. Right. A shotgun. Who has guns, he wonders. They're only used for banks. Well, he'll change all that. Right. Guns. Who? Where? Maybe he'll have to wait until dark first. The coppers would be looking for him. Fuck that. A shotgun and then they can find him. Right. Guns? Who was that guy again?

He slugs more cider. Fuck. What was his name again? He knows where to get guns. Drinks up in the Hauf Way Hoose. What was his name again? He'll take a walk over there later. Yes. Wait for dark. The Hauf Way Hoose – 'Name'll come tae me.'

This mob are in for a shock, he thinks. Coppers. Fucking wankers. They won't know what hit them. Let them come for me, he decides – 'Take wanney thum wi me.'

He crouches down in the corner. Boozers first. Get some bombers. Then back here and wait. He stares into space. This is it. No big deal, he thinks. One second and it's all over. The hours pass but seem to take forever. A lifer? Now that is forever.

'Nah. Noa fur me,' he mutters – 'Fuck, wit if es noa died?' he muses. The thought strikes a chord. Barney is an old wido after all – 'Nah, fuck it. M'noa taken any chances.'

Dawn jumps – 'Jesus! Wit? Wit is it?'

The scream startles her – 'DAWN, IT'S JOHNNY!'

Angie's hysterical – 'S'Johnny, Dawn! S'Johnny! Look! It's him! Listen!'

Dawn can't believe it. She rubs her red eyes awake.

'Oh, Jesus fuck, naw.'

Johnny's mug shot is staring from the screen. The voice-over reveals the reason: 'Police today said the man had recently been released from custody. He may also be armed. The public have been warned not to approach this man. He is extremely dangerous. We will be back after the break with the rest of the six o'clock news.'

Dawn is stunned – 'Fucksake! Right! C'mon, Angie. Get ready. C'mon. Wull huv tae catch Johnny. Time is it? Quarter-past six? Fuck, es gaun tae the fuckin George.'

Angie's in tears – 'Oh, Dawn. Oh, Dawn. Wit's gonny happen? Jesus. Johnny!'

Dawn slaps her – 'Get a fuckin grip, you! Johnny's in trouble! Noo c'mon! We need a taxi!' she snaps – 'C'mon! Wi might catch him afore they cunts dae.'

Angie pulls her coat on – 'Right, Dawn. Right. Am sorry. Right. A taxi. Wull jist get a taxi intae the toon. Maybe ey went hame furst. Es nae muney.'

Dawn slams the door behind them – 'Aye, that's right.

Naw! The George. Fuckinhell. Johnny thinks es stull alive,' she whispers – 'Fuckin fawin asleep tae, s'that hash.'

They huddle together in the middle of a taxi – 'S'that Jake's fault, so it is,' cries Angie.

Dawn nudges her leg – 'Angie! Fucksake!' she snaps – 'Shhsht. He might be listenin, fur fucksake.' She regrets it the minute it comes out, but she knows taxi drivers pass information to the police – 'Angie, look, hen,' she whispers.

Angie's face crumples up – 'Am sorry!' she bubbles.

Dawn hugs her – 'C'mon. Am sorry, hen.'

They cling to each other as the taxi driver tries to make polite conversation – 'Terrible weather, eh?'

They remain silent.

'Aye. Supposed tae be summer tae.'

Dawn draws him a look, but still he perseveres – 'Wan minute it's swelterin n the next it's ready ey rain. Too clammy fur me. George Hotel? Yes drink in there?'

She leans forward to the tiny window – 'Kin ye jist hurry up, mister?'

The driver looks in the rear-view mirror – 'Sorry, darlin. Noa take five minutes. Habit, ye know. Talkin tae ma passengers. Ye forget people huv been at wurk aw day. Jist the joab a suppose. S'borin. Drivin aboot aw day, noa wit a mean?'

Dawn can't take much more – 'Listen. Wur in a fuckin hurry, right!'

The driver gets the message this time – 'Ooops. Sorry. Wur nearly there.'

Dawn hisses – 'Fuck! Wur too late. Look.'

Police cars all over the place. They see a huge crowd outside the doors of the George Hotel.

'Bizzies are at the door. Thur aw o'er the place! Look. Wur too late.' Angie squeals – 'Aw, fuck.'

They link arms and cut through the police cars – 'Wull watch fae the bus stop. Fuckin bastards. Look at thum, the cunts.'

Angie has an idea – 'Dawn! Wull a go in an see wit's happenin?'

Dawn pulls her closer – 'Naw, hen. Ye canny.'

They stand near the lampost – 'Kin ye see um, Dawn?'

Dawn nudges her – 'Shsht.'

Jake finally has the name. Wee Shooders O'Neil! The Hauf Way Hoose! At last! He has the guy for the guns. He's halfway there. The rest is academic – 'Wee Shooders knows the score.'

He looks out the window. The street below is quiet. Darkness. Thank fuck, he thinks. Stuck in this hole all day. He makes his way down the pitch-black staircase. Rats scurry back into their holes. He kicks at them. Right. The back roads. He pulls his jacket collar up around his chin. No hurry. Walk casual. Take it easy. Don't panic. Nice and casual. He strolls into the city centre. He sees police in every car. Bastards, he thinks. His hand tightens around the handle of the razor. No problem, he tells himself. Paranoia, that's all. Relax. The Hauf Way Hoose looms up. He puts the razor up his sleeve – 'Jist incase.'

No hanging about. Get this fucking gun. Get an address and away again. He braces himself, and steps inside. The bar looks like any other bar, but that barman? This the right place? he wonders. Guy looks like a poof.

'Here you,' he shouts. The barman looks over in his

direction. Ga-wwwd, he thinks. Get hur – 'Yes? Can I help you, sir?'

Jake glares at him.

Ga-wwwd. Look at they eyes – 'Hhmmm? Would ye like a drink then?' he asks.

Jake's about to growl at him, but feels someone at his back. He slowly turns around, his head tilted – 'The fuck you daen?' he sneers.

Brogan's all teeth – 'Surprised tae see you in here, young yin. Want a pint?' he asks.

Jake's still glaring – 'Naw. Lookin fur some cunt. Wee Shoodurs. Needin a message. Fast.'

Brogan winks – 'Aint wi all. Aint wi all. Wee man's in the nick. Kinna message wis it ye wanted?' he asks.

Jake's disappointed – 'Fuck. Anythin. S'Wee Shoodurs dun fur?' he asks.

Brogan takes his arm – 'Listen. A might be able tae help ye.' The Clyde, he thinks to himself. Best place for this boy, but he has other uses – 'Get a cuppla seats, Jake. Ye huvin a pint?'

Jake lets himself be led to a table.

Brogan draws the thick wallet with the thick wad – 'Barman! Lager an a double. Shooders? Polis assaults. Six months. A wis lokin fur um maself. Ye serious aboot a message?'

Jake takes the lager – 'S'that cunt a queer?' he asks.

Brogan laughs – 'A queer? Na. Guy's bran new. Right, listen. Ye serious aboot a message? A might be able tae help ye oot.'

Jake nods his head. Why hasn't he mentioned the murder? Barney was his best pal in the jail. He takes a swallow of the pint – 'Aye. Need it the night.'

Maybe Barney isn't dead. This bampot would say something.

'How. D'ye know where a kin get wan right away?'

Brogan lifts his double – 'Fifty quid. Gie ye an address. Sawn-aff. Nae prints oan it. Ye in?' he asks.

Jake downs the lager. Fifty quid? He has about twenty quid to his name. He'll take it off whoever it is. Be a poof's gaff – 'A want ammo as well.'

Brogan doesn't ask questions – 'Fine. Right. Al phone. S'it fur a turn? Am noa askin wit yer daen. S'jist that they'll probably buy it back when yer finished.'

Jake smirks – 'Buy it back? A don't think so.'

Brogan shrugs – 'S'up tae yersel. Aw am sayin is—' He doesn't get to finish.

Jake cuts him off – 'A know wit yer sayin. Am jist tellin ye. Ye'll find oot wit it's fur shortly. Okay?'

Brogan raises his hands – 'Nae problem. Am noa wan fur questions. Anyway, al make the phone call. Ye wanta wee whisky when am up? A pint then? Okay.'

The barman passes the bar telephone over – 'A lager, didye say, Chic? Who's the guy wi the eyes?' he whispers.

Brogan twinkles and winks – 'Ye don't wanty know. Does a wee bitta graft fur me. Heavy duty, heavy duty, son.'

Brogan looks over his shoulder as he shouts into the receiver – 'Hullo? Hullo. Listen S'Big Cecil there? Oh, it's you, is it. Aye, Chic here. Witsat? Fine, fine. Listen, Cecil,' he whispers – 'S'happenin? Eh? Naw, listen. The dope. Wit's happenin wi ma dope? Wit? Listen, av payed a grand so get ma fuckin stuff. Witsat? Forgeries? Aye, that'll be fuckin right. A grand a gave ye, ya black bastard,' he hisses.

Jake takes the pint from the barman but doesn't acknowledge his presence.

'Wid ye like anything else, sir?' the barman asks – 'Eh?

Oh, well then,' he mumbles under his breath – 'Ignorant cunt.'

Jake's still staring into his pint as the barman walks away. A poof, definitely. He sips the lager. Hope his hands are clean, he thinks. He hates these fuckers – 'Poofs.'

Brogan's pressing for his payment, but no mention yet of the gun – 'Listen,' he spits into the telephone – 'Thur's a guy comin o'er in an hoor. You better huv that message ur yer in fuckin bother.' He signals the barman – 'Same again. Jake!' he calls with a thumbs up – 'S'done! A wee hauf fur the road?' Jake nods – 'Aye, okay, then.'

Brogan smiles as he sits down – 'Nae bother. Be there in an hoor? That okay? They hud a han'gun but that's away. S'a shotgun okay?' he asks out the side of his face.

Jake looks into his pint. A shotgun. Yes – 'Aye, that'll dae. S'thur bullets as well?' he asks.

Brogan raises his eyebrows – 'C'mon, young yin. S'Brogan yer dealin wi here. Think ad get ye an empty gun?' he laughs. He's in, he thinks. Cecil won't know what's hit him when he opens the door. He rubs his hands. Big black bastard. He won't try this again in a hurry. This boy's violence. Why can't he channel it into earning a serious wage, he wonders. Anyway – 'Naw, Jake. Thur's plentya ammo. Listen. V'ye never thought aboot gettin into earnin good wages? A know people that could use you fura loada joabs.'

Jake looks through him – 'A don't graft wi poofs. Where's the address?' he demands.

Brogan's too thick-skinned to take the remark personally – 'Och, Jake. Muney's muney. Ye'd make a lotta muney wi—'

Jake cuts him dead – 'Told ye. A don't graft wi—'

Brogan stammers out – 'Naw, naw. A know that Jake.

Am jist sayin that, ehm. Thur's a lotta muney fur a guy like yersel.'

Jake slams his pint down – 'A know wit yer sayin. Right. Listen. Phone these people. Tell thum am gettin a taxi, so be ready.'

He stands up to leave – 'N'by the way. This better noa be a poof's pitch. Any shite an al take the fuckin lot aff thum. S'the address again?' Brogan wishes he was going with him. He'd love to see this. Take it off them? Cecil is a six-foot transvestite. When Jake sees the dope he won't care. Give him a lump of the dope and he'll be delighted. Money could be the way to get him working. Brogan could do with back-up to make sure he gets paid.

He stands up as psycho's leaving. He's grinning – 'Jake. Listen, afore ye go. Al be here aw night. So wance ye get the thing soarted oot come back doon. Huv a cupla pints. Av somethin else ye might be interested in. Cecil's is Stonyhurst Street, Possil.'

Jake nods his head – 'Wull see. Anyway, phone, okay? A might come in later. M'noa sure wit am daen.'

He pauses a moment – 'Seen Auld Barney by the way?' he asks.

Yes, Brogan thinks. Getting Jake on board. Save a lot of problems. He's fed up with people bumping him for money all the time – 'Barney? Fucked me fur snout, the auld cunt. Heard you wur lookin fur um. Think es took off. London. V'you seen um?' he asks innocently. 'Aye, eh. Fucked me wi forgeries. Bought snout aff me. Aye, Jake. Hut me wi dummy money, the cunt. Ye noa seen um?'

Forgeries? Jake smiles – 'V'a seen um? Last time a seen um

ey wis lyin in the gutter. Anyway, mind an phone. S'this guys name again? Cecil? Right. Al see ye.'

In the gutter? Brogan frowns. Barney in the gutter? What's that supposed to mean? he wonders. He looks at his watch – 'Right. Gie this cunt wan mer warnin.'

He picks up the telephone – 'Cecil? Right, listen. That guy's oan es way o'er. Jist huv that message fur um. Noo. Ye'v been warned. Witsat?' He laughs down the line as threats erupt – 'Cecil, Cecil, Cecil. C'mon noo. Ye'll wit? Well. S'up tae yerself. Yer in bother if ye try tae threaten this guy. Am tellin ye. Wit? Listen, Cecil. Ye'v hud aw the warnins yer gonny get. S'the hospital ur gie me ma stuff.' He holds the reciever away from his ear a few moments.

'A wee whisky, Peter,' he laughs as he puts down the receiver – 'Aye. Some people never learn, dae they? Thanks, son. Wan fur yerself tae. Aye. Never learn.'

He leans over to the barman – 'See that guy? Him wi me the noo? Heavy, son. Wurks fur me ye know. A real chibman.'

The barman picks up the empty glass – 'Fine, Chic. S'ey comin back?'

Brogan adjusts his tie before heading for the door – 'Ye don't want tae get involved wi him. Too violent,' he explains – 'Aye, really violent.'

The barman purses his lips – 'Violence? Nuthin wrang wi a bitta rough.'

Brogan laughs – 'Aye eh. Anyway be back in an hoor, okay? Takin a wee donner doon ey the George. Phone a taxi fur me.'

Jake slips into the busy traffic to find a taxi. He's almost there, he thinks. He begins to wonder. Is Barney dead? He's heard nothing. Deep down he hopes he's still alive but he's taking no chances. The cops. Fuck them. He has already decided on that. A shoot-out if it comes on top. Barney though. He missed him somehow. Barney was a laugh. They'd had a lot of good times together. They'd made a lot of money too. Why did he have to grass, he wonders. Now all this. The coppers looking for him. Having to deal with a poof – 'Too fuckin late noo.'

He laughs. All those bampots you hear – how they'll go ahead with the cops when the crunch comes on top. No, he'd show them. No, they would remember him for a long time. Aye. Jake McGurk. A right game cunt. He went right ahead with the coppers. He can almost hear the conversations in his head. Jake McGurk. Game as fuck. The coppers. Jake done them. Two dead. A shotgun. Aye. They'll remember him. Jake McGurk.

He spots a taxi and whistles. The taxi turns and he gets in – 'Stonyhurst Street, up at Possil. S'the furst close oan the left. Think it's number four.'

Fifty quid? No danger. He's taking this and whatever else is there to take, he decides. Cecil? Sounds like a poof. He'll terrorise him. See if there's any money in the house. He fingers the razor. Extra cash could pay for pills – 'Get sum black bombers.'

The driver turns around – 'S'you, pal. S'two quid, mate. Right, thanks.'

Jake looks up at the windows – 'Cecil? Here we go,' he grins.

Brogan steps out of the taxi. He adjusts his tie and brushes down the camel coat. He gives himself a once-over before crossing the road to the George – 'Jesus. The fuck's this?'

The George Hotel doorway appears to be blocked by uniformed police. They are all peering over each other's shoulders to see what's going on inside the bar. Some have truncheons out while others anxiously wait for orders to move in. People are forming a crowd on the pavement, watching expectantly for something to happen – 'Wit's gaun oan? S'thur been a robbery? Wit ur the polis daen in that place?'

Police Pandas block off the traffic. Brogan weaves his way through them to watch at a distance. He stands at a lamppost outside the bar – 'S'happenin, hen?' he asks one of two girls standing in front of him.

The long-blonde-haired one throws her hair back from her face – 'Och. Jist they bastards tryin tae luft some poor guy.'

He notices the tears of the other girl – 'Ye awright, hen?' he asks. The blonde, however, nudges her to be quiet before she can say anything – 'Shsht, Angie.'

Brogan tries to look over the heads of the police but he's too small. He looks down to make sure he doesn't lose his footing as he tries to stand up on his tiptoes – 'S'that?' he mutters, noticing the faint chalk marks on the ground – 'Oh aye, young team's been busy bae the looks ey it . . .'

The two girls look down too – 'Oh, Jesus, Angie. Look. That's wit they dae when thur's been a murder. They draw aw roon the body. Ey is deid. Oh fuck. Poor, Johnny.'

Chapter Eleven

THE GARNGAD CELTIC Supporters' bus stopped at the George. The Shamrock have had a good day at Parkhead. Celtic played brilliant. Voices are hoarse from roaring and chanting rebel songs for ninety minutes at their end – The Jungle. Johnny pushes his way to the bar. The place is heaving with supporters; a sea of emerald-green scarves, bottle-green suits and green casuals – 'Tam! A lager! Right, big yin!' he shouts.

He takes a seat at one of the tables in the corner – 'Good game?' he shouts.

'Aw, Johnny, ye shooda seen thum. Pure magic.' they shout – 'HALLAUW! HALLAUW! WE ARE THE TIMALOYS! HALLAUW! HALLAUW!'

He's grinning, downing his pint – 'A wis stoned this s'mornin! Coodny make the bus!'

The table's spilling lager all over the place as the real fanatics belt out more rebel songs – 'SO-OLJURS ARE WE!' The whole bar's chanting and singing different songs – 'TO THE HOLY GROUND ONCE MORE!' There are the disputes over off-side decisions – 'MA FUCKIN ARSE!' The referee bordering on a death sentence – 'THAT ORANGE BASTARD! KNEE-CAP THAT CUNT!' In all, it's just a typical wee get together – 'HALLAUW! HALLAUW! WE ARE THE TIMALO . . . !'

A colour clash erupts as the bar is flooded with detectives, and uniformed police. They press through the bodies to reach the tables in the corner. Johnny sees them head in his direction.

All heads turn towards the commotion. Tables are knocked over as the boys from the rough ground prepare to face them down. Blades flash under jackets, steak knives appear from rolled up newspapers, tumblers are emptied onto the floor, bottles are hidden behind bottle-green jackets – 'THESE CUNTS WANT?'

When McGinty feels the hand on his shoulder he springs up, ramming the nut on the detective – BANG! – 'Fuckin hauns aff, ya prick!'

The police have been down this road before. They're trying to keep the peace. They notice they have become cut off from the door by the crowd circling them – 'Oh, c'mon noo. Calm doon. Nae need fur trouble. We jist want a word wi—' He doesn't finish his sentence – BANG! Down he goes too.

Another tries to calm things – 'Easy, lads. Thurs nae problem. Jist a word.'

McGinty's going nowhere – 'A fuckin word? Chase yer fuckin self.' He has his face pushed into the copper's – 'Ye's want fuckin trouble? Eh? Am gaun nae-fuckin-where, okay?'

The big detective smiles – 'Johnny. This kind a thing won't get us anywhere. S'jist a cuppla questions. Ye'r noa bein charged with anythin, so c'mon noo, eh?' he pleads.

McGinty looks around the bar. The silence is deadly. People will all get the jail, he thinks – 'Okay. S'it aboot then?' he demands.

The detective smiles again – 'Johnny. Ye'll be back oot in an hoor. Jist wantey clear up a wee matter. Honestly, it's jist tae clear ye fae enquiries. Ye won't even need a lawyer.'

McGinty pushes past him for the door – 'Right. C'mon en.' He looks at his pals – 'Al be back shortly. S'okay, boys. Nae trouble.'

He looks at the copper with the broken nose – 'Keep these cunts' hauns aff me ur sum cunt's gaun tae the hospital.'

The big detective knows this is not an idle threat. This is no mug – 'Nae bother, son. Nae bother. Right, let's go lads.'

McGinty recognises faces in the crowd as he bends to get into the waiting squad car. He looks up when he hears a voice call out – 'Johnny! Al visit ye!'

The big detective turns in the front passenger seat – 'Appreciate that there, son. Might have turned nasty. Gettin too auld fur this game, eh,' he smiles.

McGinty's squashed in-between two other detectives but there's no heavy stuff. They seem okay – 'Smoke, Johnny?' one asks. McGinty shakes his head – 'Nah. S'this aw aboot anyway?'

The big detective turns again – 'Och. Jist the Inspector. Wants a wee wurd wi ye. Ma name's Tom Forrest. Dinny think we've ever had any run-ins, huv wi?'

McGinty looks at him. A big bampot, he thinks – 'Nah. Don't know yer face,' he replies.

The drive to the police station is amicable; no growling. Big Tom chats to him about football, the mortgage, and the inevitable round of golf – 'Dinny suppose golf interests you, eh? Fitbaw man yerself, eh? Aye, eh.'

McGinty nods. Who is this bampot? That teuchtur accent? S'probably from the hills, he thinks – 'Aye, Cel'ic,' he replies.

Tom stares ahead, nodding – 'Aye, eh.' He looks round, slightly puzzled – 'Johnny. A meant tae ask ye. McGurk. Ever come across a laddie called McGurk? Bitty a rascal at times. Naw? Jist wondered.' He smiles at him – 'Good result the day then? Ye at the game?' he asks.

McGinty draws in his breath. Fuck. Jake. He been lifted

already, he wonders? Jake. Has he stuck him in? He stares ahead. No, they would have been heavier than this, to say the least. No. No one mentioned anything about the previous night when he was in the bar. Maybe Barney grassed Jake? Yes, this could be a pull for a statement. He begins to relax more. A statement. That's what this is all about. Yes, he smiles. That explains the softly softly approach, but he's telling them fuck all – 'Missed the bus. A wis wi a burd aw night. Knackered s'mornin.'

Tom sighs – 'Aye, eh. Big crowd in there the night, eh. The Shamrock, eh. Wild boys, a suppose. Jist the fitbaw, eh.' He laughs – 'Jings! F'Celtic had lost! Oh dearie me. A kin jist imagine they boys gaun mad, eh?'

McGinty laughs – 'The Shamrock? C'mon, big yin. They broke up ages ago.'

Tom turns, surprised – 'S'that right, John? Dearie me. N'there am thinkin they wur aw still in a gang. Aye, eh.' He jerks forward as the car pulls to a halt – 'Ooops. Well, ye grow ootey it, a suppose. Right then, lads. That's us.'

McGinty bristles as the detectives on either side grip his sleeve cuffs – 'Here. Fuck's this?' he snaps, struggling to free his arms.

Tom calms things – 'Och, Johnny. S'that desk sergeant. Geez me a timey it if a don't put the cuffs oan prisoners. S'nae need fur it either. Dinny worry,' he smiles, pushing through the door.

McGinty draws the two detectives a black look. They all know this guy can have a real go – 'Fair enough, big yin,' he drawls.

Tom smiles – 'S'nae problem, John.'

Boab doesn't look up from the property cards – 'Aye, Tom.

Inspector'll be through in a wee minute. Trouble McGinty, eh?
Right. Belt an shoe laces. Ye know the drill.'

McGinty's furious – 'Wit? The fuck ye oan aboot? M'a
gettin charged ur wit?'

Boab puts the pencil behind his ear – 'Number three. Make
sure he's kept away from other prisoners. Al gie ye a shout fur
the ID. Cuff um. Too handy wi the hauns. S'it still swelterin
oot there? Canny wait tae a get ma holidays.'

McGinty's confused – 'An ID parade? W'fur?' he demands.

Tom shakes his head – 'Shsht, John. Shsht,' he grins.

McGinty's led downstairs in handcuffs – 'A want ma fuckin
lawyer,' he shouts – 'M'a gettin charged wi sumthin?'

Anne, the turnkey, keeps her distance from him – 'Right,
then. In ye go,' she says – 'A mug a water? Right, fine. Aye,
al tell thum ye want a lawyer.'

McGinty hears the door slam behind him. Bastards, he
thinks. What the fuck's going on? An ID parade? What
for? He hasn't done anything. He paces up and down. An
ID? He can't fathom it out. An ID? Stay calm, he tells
himself. Stay cool. Don't let them see the confusion. What
can it be though? That big bampot being all nice. The big prick
knows. They're pulling a stroke, he thinks. There's something
he's missing, something he can't see.

He slows down the pace. Think, he thinks. Think hard.
What the fuck are they up to? He kicks the door – 'Bastards!'

Jerry's holding Karen's hand in the canteen – 'Don't worry.
We'll be right beside ye,' he assures her – 'McGinty's wearin
a blue denim shurt.'

Karen's blonde wig hides most of her face. Nothing, however, can conceal the terrible scar along her cheekbone; time

may heal as the say, but those deeper scars are there forever, terrors that haunt her sleep, a meat cleaver from behind. These things are rarely, if ever, forgotten – 'Al be fine, Jerry.'

Tom comes bounding in – 'Karen! They wantye tae come doon noo. The parade's aw ready. Dinny worry noo. Jerry's right beside ye. Al be watchin tae. Ye dinny huv tae worry anymer, darlin.'

They all head downstairs to a brightly lit corridor – 'Al be fine, Tom.'

McGinty is standing in the middle of the line of men. He's staring ahead as she walks down, looking at each of the faces. He's never seen her before. Check that Mars Bar, he thinks. Karen stops before him, scrutinising his face. He smirks when he hears her say – 'No. S'noa him. Am sorry.'

Jerry's disappointed, but not that you would notice – 'Okay, lads. Take him through to the bar.'

When McGinty laughs in his face, he grins – 'Inspector's waitin there. Aye eh, think yer a wido, McGinty. Ye mighta got away way chibbin a wumin but yer no gonnae walk ootey the urra wan, son.'

Tom waves through – 'Bring um through noo. Inspector's there noo,' he calls.

McGinty swaggers through to the bar to pick up his property. An Inspector? A wind up, he thinks.

Jerry's right behind him, giggling – 'The big shot, eh,' he mocks.

McGinty freezes; his brain hears the words, but can't take them in. The Inspector is charging him with murder – 'John McGinty,' he catches snippets, but understands it fully – '. . . Charged with . . .' He feels his stomach fall through the floor – 'murdering Saab Patel . . .' He doesn't believe this – 'You have the right to remain silent.' He feels hands on him as he's led away to the holding cell.

'Lock im up, Sergeant.'

Saab Patel? Who the fuck is he? his brain is screaming. Saab Patel? Fuck! There was that guy, that Paki. Saab! That was it. Murdered? When? He still can't fathom what is happening when the door slams behind him. What the fuck is going on? Barney. He believed this was connected to him. What the fuck is this? Nothing made any sense. The bird, too, with the scar. What was that all about? He'd never seen her before, and now this, charged with murdering this Paki?

Murder. Jesus. He is in trouble. Murder. The word echoes around his head. He can't think. Murder. Life. How can it be murder? He hasn't murdered anyone? He shakes his head. Why didn't they mention Barney? He must be alive, right enough. Jake, he thinks. Where is he? This is all that bampot's fault. He would be out if he had stayed out of the fight. He should never have jumped in. If only he had turned away, or if he had stayed in the bar he would have missed the fight altogether. But this Paki? What is happening? The last time he saw him was in the cells. That fat prick had taken him away but he must have got bail, he never came back. Did Jake kill him? Jake! That bastard was after the guy. That's what's happened. It's been that bastard!

Karen's apologetic – 'Naw, honestly. Av never seen him before. Naw, it wis that other guy, him wi the blue eyes,' she shudders.

Tom holds her hand – 'Dinny you worry yerself. Wis jist on the off-chance that he wis there. S'McGurk wur lookin fur.

O'Hara's in the nut hoose,' he answers – 'But dinny you worry. We'll find him.'

Jerry laughs – 'Didye see McGinty? Anurra fuckin ned. Boab won't let me near um,' he boasts – 'A hard case, ma arse.'

Tom looks down at his coffee – 'Aye, eh. Terrible kerry-oan that,' he murmurs.

Karen looks at him – 'Wit did he dae? Assault somebody?' she asks.

Jerry goes into hysterics laughing – 'Sorry, Karen. McGinty? Aye. Battered the Paki doon the cells. Poor cunt died as a result. A vicious bastard, that yin,' he states – 'No be batterin anymer Pakis noo, eh, big man?'

Tom gets up from the table – 'Right, Karen. Al drive ye back hame then.' He turns to his partner – 'Well, Jerry, McGinty didny gie me any trouble. A dinny understuan why ye've got it in fur him. Es noa like the rest ey that crowd.'

Jerry laughs – 'Aw, Tom, c'mon! Yer noa gettin soft ur ye? McGinty's an animal. The cunt broke wanney oor boys' noses the night. Wit aboot him? Who backs him then? Naw, c'mon noo, big yin. McGinty's done fur that poor Pakistani chappie. Noa that es any great loss, but ye canny let these people jist go aboot murdurin people.'

Tom offers no resistance. Jerry's right – *isn't he*. They had to stick together in the field, but the boy downstairs troubled him – 'Aye, well. Ye right, Karen?'

Karen's aware of the silence in the car. She'd known this man long enough now to sense when something was bothering him. This deeply shy man had terrible difficulty hiding anything from her – 'Tom? S'there somethin the matter?' she asks.

Tom frowns over the wheel – 'Well, eh. There's something.

Eh, something's noa right at aw. That man's, eh, innocent,' he stammers out – 'He coodnae huv dun it . . .'

Karen's confused – 'Wit man? Who're ye talkin aboot? That McGinty?' she persists.

Tom blurts out the whole lot – 'Aye, Karen. A didny join the police service fur this. Av never told lies, Karen. A know wit we did wis wrang, huvin an affair n that, but av telt Maureen. The divorce'll finalise things, but this?' He takes a deep breath – 'Karen, it wis Jerry.'

Karen's stunned – 'Jerry? A don't understaun. Jerry killed somebody? My God, Tom, ur ye serious?' she exclaims. She knows, though, that this man would never lie – 'God, Tom. How dae ye know? A know that ey kin be a bit heavy-handed but murder? How did it happen?'

Tom's conscience spills out – 'Auld Boab wis in oan it as well. Jerry beat up that man in the cells. A wis away gettin tea ur somethin. Mind when es troosers came loose up at the Woodside? Well, a suspected somethin then. When ey came tae see me up at the hospital ey told me wit happened.'

He describes the friendship in the past tense, she notices. He has his mind made up already.

'Karen. A canny jist staun by an watch. This isnae right. They were sayin it wis suicide at first. Then they decided tae blame that laddie. Av hardly slept wi worry. A jist want ye tae know. Am tellin the truth.'

Karen touches his arm – 'Oh, Tom. Be careful. Ye know wit thur like. N'Jerry's liked doon there. N'Boab tae. That's a nasty auld swine. Oh, Tom.' She reaches over and kisses his cheek – 'Ye'r a decent man. Ye know al staun by ye no matter wit happens. But ye must tell the truth, Tom.'

Tom smiles reassuringly – 'Aw, dinny worry. When

McGurk's caught, am resignin fae the force. A jist coodny work wi this oan ma mind. Dearie me, eh. Jerry's went too far this time. Well, it's murder,' he admits – 'Aye eh. When McGurk's behind bars al haun in ma resignation. McGinty's a rogue, but he disnae deserve this. Murder's the worst kind.'

He feels relieved to get it off his chest – 'Jerry's been a pal, but there's a bad side tae es nature. Something perverted like. Ey enjoys the violence. Av seen it fur maself. Eyes shinin, an gettin aw o'er excited. S'noa right. People need a chance sometimes. Thur noa aw bad. So am resignin.'

Karen knows that once his mind is made up there's no going back – 'Oh, Tom. Well, ye kin huv the pub wi me. Av got ma pension as well. We'll be fine thegither.' The wound on her face tingles – 'Aye. Ye must tell the truth. Tom. Kin a ask ye somethin?'

Tom looks at her a moment – 'Aye, Karen. Wit is it?'

She looks down at the floor of the car – 'Ma face, Tom.'

Tom tries to turn away – 'Aw, Karen, am so sorry, saw ma fault,' he sighs – 'Jerry tae. That McGurk'll show up, but we shooda known he'da came back tae the pub that day. Karen, am so sorry, hen. Ye'r a braw lookin wumin. A don't see the scar when a look at you. Och, ye'r an awful wumin so ye ur. Jings. Wit aboot ma big ugly mug?' he says, taking her hand – 'Aye, eh. Always tell the truth. We shood nevera come tae the pub. It was the money ey was after, Jerry.'

Karen grips his hand – 'Oh, Tom, don't blame yourself for this.'

Chapter Twelve

MCGINTY PULLS HIMSELF together. There's nothing he can do. Panicking won't resolve anything. He's paces up and down the floor. The best thing to do is wait until he can get a visit. Dawn and Angie will find out what's going on. Barney though. Is he dead or alive? Did Jake kill him or what? Did Jake kill this Pakistani guy?

He tries to make sense of the facts. The facts? Fu-ck. Charged with murdering a guy. That's the fucking facts, he laughs. Je-sus. Did Jake have time? What if he had done the Paki? What if he had looked for the guy. Could he have killed him? Fuck. What if?

He sits down in a corner. Try to think, he thinks. Try to place people. Barney. Jake. Where are they? he wonders. If Barney is dead, why haven't they questioned him on that? The Pakistani? What the fuck is that all about? Jake. Where is he? Has Jake been charged too? The George Hotel was packed, but was he there? That big prick, he asked if he knew him. That's right. So they must be looking for him, surely?

He lies down on the floor, staring at the bricks. Jesus, he thinks. Nothing is making a bit of fucking sense. He gets up, and begins pacing the floor. He counts the steps to the door and retraces them back to the wall. Ten steps. What was that film again? he wonders. *The Thirty-Nine Steps*. That's it. Fuck, he thinks. Concentrate, think, for fucksake. He lies back down, and closes his eyes. Murder. Life. Jesus. He hears the words rattling through his head. That bastard, he swears. He'll kill him if this is down to him, but the Pakistani? Did Jake kill the guy? What if Barney? Was it *Thirty-Nine?*

McGinty stirs in the morning. He sees the bulb's dim light outside the door first. The door clangs open – 'Wash an breakfast,' someone snaps. He gets up, not sure where he is before it hits him. Murder. Life. His stomach flips. Jesus. He has difficulty for a moment. Putting on a face isn't what he has in mind. He hears the breakfast barrow wheels squeaking towards his cell – 'Breakfast,' the voice snaps – 'Ye want breakfast, ur jist a muggatea?'

McGinty opens the buttered roll and almost vomits. The plastic egg inside is covered in grease. He looks inside the other to find a thick raw sausage. A cigarette is what's foremost in his mind, but he won't ask the turnkey. That's for bams. He takes a dirty plastic mug, and dips it into the tea urn without a word.

The turnkey looks inside the cell – 'That you then?' he snaps. Bang! The cell door slams.

'Pricks.' McGinty mutters.

Panic. That's what they watch for. Panic and questions. He's too wide for that. The tea is tasteless, but gives him something to do. He hunches down in the corner. The time, he wonders. Must be about six, knowing these bastards, he thinks. He begins to walk up and down – slowly at first, but within an hour he's pacing the length of the cell, his brain racing. The Sheriff Court. They'll take him there first, commit him for trial. Fuck, he thinks. A hundred-and-twelve-day lie-down in Barlinnie. He dreads to think of the bottom landing of C-hall. The row of capital charges awaiting trial. All of them with their heads nipping. All of them convinced of a 'not guilty', or at least a 'not proven' – 'Al fuckin kill that prick fur this,' he swears.

*   *   *

The Sheriff Court is heaving when he finally makes the brief appearance to make his first plea. The lawyer representing him mutters the 'no plea' declaration. McGinty's looking straight at the Sheriff as he remands him into custody, pending a full commital in seven days. Fuck, he thinks. Back down here again next week. Stuck in those tin cans downstairs.

He looks over his shoulder towards the public gallery. He smiles as he sees Dawn and Angie. They're huddled together in the middle of all those worried faces. He frowns. Angie's making exaggerated movements with her mouth. He tries to follow the lip contortions. What's she saying? he wonders. He turns back to face the court – 'Remanded into custody. Next.'

McGinty is led away by two uniformed policemen. He shrugs his shoulders as they're passing the line of faces. What? Angie's on her feet – 'Al visit ye,' she calls.

He laughs, shaking his head. Jesus. She never gives up. Still, they were at court and may even be able to find out what's happening. He blows them a kiss – 'Dun ur fuckin nut, eh Dawn!' he calls.

Dawn smiles, but her face is drawn – 'Don't worry, Johnny. Al be up tae see ye. Send a visit pass.'

He turns away as he sees the tears – 'Nae borra, hen! Send wan fur next week, okay!'

The two policemen return him to the court holding-cage. He sits in the corner to wait for the Barlinnie van. The cage is tiny. Two steps. One forward, and one back. The seat is the only option. Skud's name is dug into a wall. Fuck, he thinks. Tripping on acid, and still cuts his monocle into the brick – 'Fuckin headcase.'

He sits staring through the bars. No point trying to think now, he decides. He tries to blot out the noise; people screaming for water, cigarettes, and demands to see their briefs – 'BOSS! BOSS! HERE YOU, YA FUCKIN PRICK! S'NAE FUCKIN WATER! HERE YOU, YA FUCKIN BAM! AM UP YER WIFE, YA CUNT! WIT? A NEVER SHOUTED! YERA BIG POOF, YA CUNT! WIFE TAKES IT UP THE ARSE, YA CUNT! ANY WATER? EH? AV NOA SHOUTED, YA CUNT YE! BOSS?'

McGinty listens to the racket, promising to batter every one of them when he sees the first opportunity.

A turnkey appears at the door – 'Dinner.'

McGinty takes the two sandwiches. He swallows the one with spam. The other with the plastic cheese, he skites along the small corridor at a cell door. The plastic cup is scalding hot, almost impossible to hold, but he manages to get the tea down. Fuck, a fag, he thinks. He'd kill for a drag right now. His head is pounding; withdrawals, that endless shouting, the banging. Surely there's an early van to the jail, but no. He sits there in the cage for around eight hours before being herded into the van with all the jakeys and serious faces.

'Any cunt got fags?' he asks.

The guy behind passes him a roll-up – 'You the guy dun fur the murdur, pal?' he asks.

McGinty twists round to look at the face – 'Aye, how?'

The broken face looks back at him through watery eyes – 'Naw. A jist heard ye wur dun wi murdur. Take a couple a smokes, pal. Wull get fuck all up here. You'll need thum mer than me, pal.'

McGinty thanks him and sticks the extras into the lining of

his jeans – 'Aye. Murdur an two polis assaults. Thanks, pal. Ye dun fur?'

The broken face dismisses the question – 'Ach, a daft breach. Aye, heard they copper cunts laughin. You McGinty? Aye, they wur aw laughin. Ye fae the Garngad? Used tae steal coal up there, up Blackhull. Dae ye know the Morrisons?' he asks.

McGinty takes in a lungful of tar – 'S'better,' he sputters – 'Fuckinhell man. Ye goat in that? Straw?' he laughs – 'S'that Wullie an Tot Morrison? Aye, a know thum,' he says – 'Game cunts, they two. S'your name by the way?'

Handcuffs rattle as they shake hands – 'Och, ye won't know me, mate. M'jist a thief. A used tae stay in Blackhull. The faimly moved tae Govan. Wine Alley. Aw, sorry. Tam Burns. Tommy, aye. You're Johnny, intye. Aye, av heard ey ye. Shamrock, eh.'

McGinty enjoys the escape from his head – 'S'at right? Dae a owe ye muney? Thank fuck fur that, eh,' he laughs.

Tam passes his lighter – 'Here, Johnny. Ye better hide it. They cunts don't let murdur raps keep lighters in thur peturs. Cunts settin thumselves oan fire an at. Al get snout doon tae ye wance wur in the halls,' he promises.

McGinty's grateful – 'Thanks, Tam. A think al walk. Dun me wi a fuckin Paki. Never touched the fuckin guy. Naw, ey wis doon the cells and then—'

Tam interrupts – 'That the guy they fun in the cells? Heard aboot it. S'it noa you? We aw heard ey got battured. S'oan the news. Said it wis a prisnur.'

McGinty sits up – 'Oan the news? Wid they say?' he asks – 'Listen. V'ye heard ey an auld guy, Barney Boone?'

Tam laughs – 'Auld Barney? Ye kiddin. Here, that's right. Some cunt dun um. Up at the George. Stabbed in the neck ur sumthin, am noa sure. Heard thur lookin fur sum guy fae up your way, up the Garngad.'

McGinty can't believe his luck in finding Tam – 'Wit? R'ye kiddin? So es definitely deid? Ye sure it wis a guy fae the Garngad? Wisnae McGurk, wis it?' he prays.

Tam's an angel – 'Aye! That's him! McGurk! Coodny remember es fuckin name. Ye know um?' he asks.

McGinty praises him – 'Aw, Tam, ya fuckin beauty. The coppers lookin fur um? Great! Cunt drapped me right innit. S'a long story. How dae ye know they're lookin fur um? S'that definite?'

Tam knows this guy's desperate for information – 'Aw, it's definite, mate. Coppers wur gaun mental lookin fur um the urra night,' he explains – 'Some cunt seen um. Aye, a witness saw um runnin away wi a blade ur sumthin,' he explains.

McGinty's grinning from ear to ear – 'Aye, Tam. Canny tell ye anymer, okay. Ye'v dun me a favour, pal, honest. Wit aboot the Paki? Wid ye hear there?' he begs.

Tam's delighted to be the bearer of good news – 'The wee Paki?' He frowns, trying to remember exactly what he'd heard – 'Wull, the rumour is that it wis the coppers,' he says – 'A cuppla young boys heard aw the kerry-oan an at. Next thing the guy's deid. Then they heard you wur dun fur it. Coppers slung the young boys oot. PF's release.'

McGinty can't believe it. That fat bastard killed the guy. He tries to think, but the bus is too noisy.

'Tam,' he says, 'Ye'v dun me a real favour, mate. A jist coodny work oot wit hud happened. Bastards. Aw, al be walkin, but they dun that poor cunt fur nuthin. Guy wis bran new. Fuckin liberty. Listen, a might get ma lawyer tae talk tae ye. S'at okay?'

Tam's all excited – 'Wit? Aye! Fucksake, man. Ye kiddin? Gie um ma name. Al talk tae um, nae bother. That's how a asked ye who ye wur. Every cunt's talkin aboot it. A canny see ye even daen the full lie-doon.'

McGinty is overwhelmed with relief. He knows nothing can happen to him now. The very worst is a lie-down in the untried hall, but they'll never convict him now that he's found credible witnesses.

'Right, Tam. Look, wur nearly there. Al get ma lawyer tae see ye, okay. Fuck me, man. A canny believe this.'

Tam's only glad he can be of help – 'Nae borra, Johnny. Al gie ye ma maw's address. Jist incase, an al gie the lawyer a statement. A know the boys that wur in the cells tae, so nae problem mate, okay.'

Johnny lurches forward as the van swings into the main drive of Barlinnie.

'Aw, Tam. Yer a fuckin diamond, pal. Anythin a kin dae fur ye jist geez a shout.'

Tam blushes – 'Ach, fuck. Nae borra, man. See ye the morra at exercise, okay.'

A screw in a white medic coat ushers the passengers into the reception area. They all line up to see the doctor outside the surgery. No one speaks. Not a sound is uttered. They know that the wrong look or a remark can result in having their heads shaved for supposed lice. Any lip guarantees a severe battering.

The doctor's voice is the only sound – 'Religion? Ever had measles, typhoid, or any other illness? Right, drop yer pants. Any crabs? Right, bend over. Okay. Next.'

McGinty knows the drill. He swaggers through the 'Dog Boxes'. He doesn't mind that they are three-feet square, and already housing two other prisoners. They are eating from plastic bowls as he's locked in with them. The noise level resumes until screws begin the rounds.

'Here! You daen the shoutin?' Bang! – 'Shut it, okay!'

The boxes fall silent for a few minutes then gradually build up to shouting level, until – 'Here! Ye fuckin deaf, son?' Bang! – 'Keep the fuckin noise doon!'

McGinty squeezes into the box with the two other guys – 'Fucksake, eh!' he laughs, a bit loudly.

He's turning round as the door opens. The screw in the white coat glares inside at the occupants.

'You fuckin stupit, son?'

McGinty's ready for it. Bang! The screw lands up against the opposite door, his nose broken.

'HELP! ASSISTANCE! AM BEIN ASSAULTED!' he's squealing.

McGinty's walking. He's bursting to batter more of them. Two more white coats turn red. Bang! Bang! He's battered from behind. The crunching noise of a riot stick hits his ears first, before the blood spouts all over his face.

The screw's startled when the prisoner spins round and punches him out cold.

Yes, he's walking. He's not giving a fuck, even when he's overpowered and battered, he's still walking.

They drag him to C-hall. The padded cell is waiting for him, but so what – he's walking. They throw him in and lock the door.

'Wait tae thur aw locked up. See this cunt en,' a voice says, but the unconscious prisoner doesn't give a fuck – he's definitely walking.

McGinty comes round again – 'Bampots,' he sniggers. He

pulls the lighter and a roll-up from the lining of his jeans.

'Pricks. Ahhh. S'better,' he sighs. Tam's face looms up. Wee Tam, his new best pal.

'They durty bastards,' he murmurs. They killed that poor guy. He promises himself to visit the guy's family. Tell them the truth about their brother, or son, being murdered in a police station. The dirty murdering bastards. He will bring it all out at the trial. He can't wait to have the trial now that he knows. The coppers are in for trouble, he thinks. Murdering that guy in a cell? The bastards. Did they think they would get away with it?

He hears a muffled shout from outside the cell – 'Ri-ight! Lock-u-p! C'mon then! Get thum ahint thur doors!'

He knows they will be coming in after the lock-up. He hides the lighter while taking a last drag – 'Here we go,' he smiles.

Big 'Bootsie' Macmillan fills the door when it's thrown open – 'Right then, son. Bitty a ticket ur wi?' he asks mildly.

McGinty's in the corner, but far from cowering – 'How, you gonny tober me up?' he smiles.

The 'Boot' takes his name from the first pair of platform boots ever designed for a stunted personality. His big, blue jawbone grits into an even bigger clenched jawbone.

'Oh, wuv a ticket here, lads,' he smiles over a shoulder – 'Well, we canny huv tickets in here noo, kin wi, lads?'

The pack waiting at his back are slavering at the mouth – 'Na-aw. Nae tickets in here,' they drool – 'Na-aw, we're the tickets in this place.'

The 'Boot' throws his hat off – 'Right then, son. S'jist me

an you. C'mon then, son. Av ma tea tae get hame tae. S'wullny take long.'

McGinty learned to fight in the street as a boy. He's been a fighter all his life. He hangs loose as he watches this bampot's tactics to catch him off-guard with all the hamming. He moves forward and pulls the same stunt – 'Ye gonny staun there aw night?' he drawls.

The 'Boot' falls for it – 'Eh? Wit wis tha—'

Bang! He's knocked out. McGinty knows this is as far as he gets with the square-go lark. They're climbing over each other to get at him with their sticks.

'Get um! That's it! Haud um doon! That's it! That's it!'

McGinty hears those crunching noises again; the colours spinning round, and round, and round.

Whack! Bang! Bang! – 'Haud um! The bastard! Haud um doon!' but he doesn't give a fuck, he's walking.

He falls into black unconsciousness. He's been here before. A few bumps and bruise marks in the morning. No big deal. He's dished it out, so he has no complaint. They have to retaliate. He knows that. Anyway – he's walking.

When he comes round he rolls over, pulls out the lighter and sighs – 'Ahhh. S'better. Fuckin bampots,' he laughs. He fingers his scalp – 'Probably need a cuppla stitches noo. Oh well. Ahhh. S'much better,' he sighs, exhaling the wonderful smoke.

The light of his cell remains on the whole night, but he doesn't mind at all because he has no fears. Jake, he thinks. He's in trouble. Jake can't possibly grass him now they are both going to be in the untried together. Jake he knows won't last long out there now he's on his own. Dawn was right about him. He can't do anything without mates. A lifer too, he smiles.

He'll never handle that, probably commit suicide, the prick. Well, Jake, that's the way it goes. You're on your own this time – 'Jist yer fuckin luck.'

McGinty drifts off into sleep. He remains there all night undisturbed by nightmares. He feels stiff from the beating the night before, but, well, he's not too bothered. He wolfs down the bowl of porridge, and enjoys the big thick slices of bread. Barlinnie has the best bread in the country. Prisoners survive in this place on cheese, bread and tea. He lights a roll-up – 'Ahhh. S'better. Wonder'f thurs any extra breed?'

The screw hands in more bread – 'How ye feelin? Bootsie's no happy. Said ye'v goat a fair dig. Anyway, ye okay noo? Get ye washed an o'er tae the surgery later. Might need a cuppla stitches. Anyway, there's the paper. Nae mer kerry-oan, okay?'

McGinty smiles – 'Ach, nae borra, boss. Heid wis nippin that wis aw. Listen, how dae a get tae ma lawyer?' he asks.

The screw leaves him at the cell door. He picks up a letter from the desk – 'Here. Dae a visit pass. Al get it away this s'mornin. Yer lawyer oan the phone? S'the number? Al get thum tae contact es office, okay? Right, mind the visit pass. In ye go.'

Dawn and Angie recieve the visit pass a few days later – 'Oh look, Angie. S'a pass fur Johnny. S'fur the morra efternin.'

Angie reads the slip of paper – 'Oh, that's magic, Dawn. A wisnae sure if they wid get visits. A wunder if ye kin take anythin in tae um? A cake ur somethin? Bet the food's terrible in that place.'

Dawn pulls cigarette papers to build another joint – 'Naw. Don't be daft. They'd hink thur wis a file innit. Anyway, am gled you've cheered up a bit. S'beginning tae wunder there fur a minute.'

Angie puts the visit pass into her bag – 'Ach. A like Johnny, Dawn. Es noa like the rest ey thum. Es a good guy so ey is.' She puts the kettle on – 'Tea, Dawn? Dawn. Kin a ask ye somethin?' She doesn't wait for a reply – 'R'ye really missin Skud? Wull, kin wi noa goan see um then? S'a shame, so it is. Skud never really dun anythin. Takin a tab ey acid? Lookit Jake. He killed that auld man an es stull walkin the streets. It's noa fair, is it?'

Dawn agrees – 'Naw, a know Angie. But look, Skud dun es ain thing. Am definitely noa gain near that place. Wit wid a say tae um? A mean, es mad.'

She takes Angie into the scullery – 'Angie, look, hen. Johnny might get a lifer here. Barney's deid. So the best thing tae dae is try tae get oan wi things. Thurs a lotta guys runnin aboot the toon so don't get caught up wi aw this jail thing. It'll dae yer heid in, honest.'

They sit staring into their cups in silence.

Angie turns to her – 'A wis rajin in court the urra day. They fuckin polis aw laughin. Didye see that fat wan staunin there? Him wi the snide look aw the time? A felt ded sorry fur Johnny.'

She lifts her head – 'Dawn? Right, listen. Right. A know wit yer gonny say. Am gonny wait fur um. Johnny's in trouble. Ey needs somebody. Right, okay, ey might noa thingmy. But, am gonny visit um. Ye must need somebody in they places. A visit wid keep um gaun. Anyway, it's the least a kin dae fur the guy. They bastards laughin at um an es innocent.'

Dawn's surprised by her determination – 'Okay, fair enough. Johnny is a good guy. A know wit ye mean. A saw that fat cunt laughin tae. Nevermind. Wull jist huv tae wait an see wit ey says furst an then we kin try an help. A might go a witness fur um. Say it wis Jake. A noa it's grassin, but . . .'

Angie perks up – 'Aye! Me tae. A wis thinkin aboot that last night. Means people'll a know'll call me a grass but a don't care.'

Dawn has the same concerns – 'A know, but yer right, it wis that other bastard that caused aw this. Skud tae. Right, wull see wit ey says when wi go up tae see um the morra.'

Angie's elated – 'Oh, Dawn. Be great tae get um oot, wint it? See aw they polis. They'd be sick. That bastard that wis daen aw the laughin when ey wis in the court.'

Angie remembers his face – 'That bastard. Aye, Angie. That's wit wull dae. Johnny's done nuthin. Al tell um furst. You get nervous an at. Really fancy um dint ye? Don't worry, hen. See who's laughin when ey gets a not guilty.'

Chapter Thirteen

JERRY HAD INDEED been laughing. He had gone down to the court on his own to watch McGinty. Big Tom had declined. He was worried about the big man. Something was on his mind. He was avoiding him. McGinty, though, that was a laugh. He looked the part, all that bravado – 'Bampot. Huv tae huv a word wi Tam,' he decides.

He looked at his watch – two-thirty. He decides to look in at the station to see if there was any sign of him – 'Where is ey?' he wonders.

Three detectives sitting at a table call out – 'Jerry! Ye got a wee minute. Somethin ye might find interestin,' they laugh.

Jerry's curious to hear the joke – 'S'happenin en, lads?' he smiles – 'Seen Big Tam in at aw?'

They look around – 'Naw, Jerry. Ye meetin um here? We've been here fur a wee while, the big man's definitely noa been in. Anyway. V'ye heard the latest?'

Jerry can't believe his ears – 'Wha-aat? McGurk? Naw. Yer kiddin!' he roars. They tell him it's the truth.

'Fun deid last night. Aye, an wait tae ye hear this.'

Jerry can't believe it. O'Hara in the nut house. McGinty lying in Barlinnie. Auld Barney snuffed out. And now this. McGurk murdered?

'When? Where aboots? Right. Give me the details, an take yer time boys. Av waited a long time fur this.'

The detective on the case elaborates – 'Aye, heard ye wur gunnin fur um. Well, Jerry boy, we got um furst!' He hunches over the table – 'Right. Well, we're oan a call. Up at Possil. Some headcase screamin thurs been a murder. Right? So, me an Andy. A cuppla uniforms, fire up tae the hoose. Stonyhurst Street. Right? So thurs naibidy in. A take a look aboot an er ey is. Sprawled o'er the livin room fler.'

Jerry can't contain himself – 'McGurk! Ya fuckin beauty. Right, so wit happened?'

The detective grins – 'Right. A look in the livin room and aw ye kin see is an arse! Aw, ye won't believe this. Right? Thurs an arse! Stuck up in the air! "Andy," a shouts, "wid ye take a look at this." Andy bursts oot laughin tae. Honest, a coodny believe it. There ey is, smilin! Gen up! Paira tights roon es neck! Aye! Smilin!' he roars.

Jerry's mouth is hanging wide open – 'Jesus Christ. A knew it. A poof. Ye kin spot it a mile away.'

The other detective butts in – 'Aye, but haud oan. That's noa aw. Naw, wait tae ye hear this. Es fuckin bollocks naked! Aye! Gen up! Right? Next thing av phoned the *Daily Record*. Gave thum the full spiel. Yes, the police believe that the motive is sexual. The evidence was "loaded" with sexual connotations.'

Jerry interrupts again – 'Loaded? Widye mean?' he giggles.

Andy interjects – 'Arse wis stuffed wi a wadda banknotes! Aw rolled up! Like a Swiss-fuckin-Roll!'

The whole table bursts into hysterics – 'Aye! Honest! Loaded! That's nuthin. S'aw forgeries! Honest! Tight-arsed cunt, eh!' he roars.

Jerry's trousers are at bursting point with excitement. He can't believe it.

'McGurk eh! A-w, av waited a long time for this!'

He looks up from the table – 'T-am! C'mere tae ye hear this!' His voice trails off. What's this? he wonders.

Tom's face is ashen as he comes over — 'Jerry. Chief Inspector wid like tae see ye,' he says solemnly.

The Chief Inspector is there in his office with two other detectives. Jerry's never seen them before. They don't look too happy. He senses something wrong — 'S'everything okay, Tam?' he asks.

One of the detectives reads from a serious-looking sheet of paper — 'Jeremy P. Mahony, sir? There's a matter we have to discuss, Mr Mahony,' he says sternly.

Jerry's confused — 'Afternoon, Inspector. S'there a problem?' he asks with a growing bewilderment. The detective takes him by the elbow in what's obviously an arrest.

'Eh? Wit? Tam? S'happenin here, mate?' he stammers.

Is it an accident? Karen? Auld Boab? Jerry's panicking — 'S'there something a need tae know?' he croaks. He lets himself be led downstairs. An accident? Karen? God, no. What's happened.

'Tom? S'the matter. Tell me,' he pleads.

Tom remains silent until they reach the bar. Where's Boab? Jerry wonders. Boab. Is he dead? A heart attack or something? God, not bad news — 'Tam. C'mon. Give it to me straight.'

The Inspector stands abreast of Jerry and Tom. He folds his arms and nods. The two other detectives move to either side of Jerry. Tom looks straight into his eyes with an ice-cold stare he'd never seen before. 'Jeremy P. Mahony. You are charged with the murder of Saab Patel. You have the right to remain silent. Anything you say may be used against you in a court of law. You have the right to a lawyer . . .'

Jerry feels his legs buckle — 'Oh, Jesus Christ. Oh, Jesus Christ, no. Aw, c'mon. Tam, wit ye playin it, man? A huvny killed anybody . . .' he spits, snapping — 'Ya fuckin rats bastard!

You won't get away wi this!' he screams – 'S'a fit up! S'a fit up, ya big fuckin rat ye!'

The Inspector nods again – 'Take im away,' he says, turning to Tom – 'Fine, son. You have done well. I will not tolerate this type of officer in my force. There is no room in the force for these types.'

Tom turns to leave, his head bowed, but the Inspector has one more thing to say – 'It has been brought to my attention that you are seeking a promotional post. Well, well well. Let's sort this out first. I'm recommending a transfer to Edinburgh. You've done very well at this station. It would be a pity to lose your experience. Still. Right, then. A day at home wouldn't do any harm. Off you go and well done, Forrest.'

Tom drags himself to the door – 'Thank you, sir.' He fills his lungs with fresh air. God, what a day, he thinks. Karen waves from the car. He joins her.

'Well? How did it go in there?' she asks.

Tom turns the engine on – 'We've charged thum wi that man's murder. McGinty'll be released the day at some point. They'll have tae drop aw they other charges. Dearie me. McGinty's assaulted two policemen. Awful man. Anyway. How dae ye fancy us livin in Edinburgh? Yer talkin tae Deputy Chief Inspector Tom Forrest.'

Karen laughs, for the first time in a long time it seems – 'Aw, Tom. Ye dun the right thing,' she cries – 'Yev dun the right thing.'

Tom swings the car out of the station. He glances up at the cell windows – 'Oh, dearie me. How wull they survive prison? Aw they boys they two battered. Auld Boab, tae. They'll jist retire him. Aye, eh. Well, Edinburgh it is,' he smiles.

*   *   *

McGinty's staring at the ceiling when the cell door opens.

'McGinty. Reception. Ye got any gear tae take wi ye?' the screw asks.

McGinty jumps up – 'Gear? Ye talkin aboot?'

The screw shrugs – 'Dunno. Ye expectin bail ur anythin?' he asks.

McGinty's belly flutters with butterflies – 'Bail? Nah. Am expectin a visit.'

The screw locks the door behind them – 'Well. The reception want ye right away,' he says. He turns to the desk – 'Right. One off! Reception!'

The 'Boot' looks up from the desk. He puffs out his chest – 'Aye, then. Be anurra time, McGinty,' he smiles.

McGinty looks at him. He can't keep the smile off his face – 'Al break yer jaw next time, big yin.'

The 'Boot' waves him off – 'Ach, dinny kid yersel, laddie. Next time it'll be the gloves. Anyway get the fag oot. Yer noa oot yet, McGinty.'

McGinty flicks the roll-up away. Out? – 'Aye, right,' he laughs.

The reception area is a blur. McGinty pulls on his clothes. A screw calls him to the desk.

'Right, sign here.'

Next thing he's walking through to the front gate house. He passes the visitors' waiting room. Some screws are looking under seats before letting the visitors inside.

'Right!' one calls through the desk – 'Let thum in.'

McGinty brushes past the stream of visitors coming through the gate – 'Oops! Sorry, hen. Oops! Right, son. Sorry there, hen. Jesus. Kin ye let me oot? Thanks. Oops! Sorry, hen. Right then – YEEEEEEEEEEEES!'

Dawn and Angie are waiting outside the gate with the other visitors – 'Wit a kerry-oan, eh. Staunin here fur fuckin two hoors. Es furst visit tae,' they moan.

Angie sees him first – 'Dawn! Look! Dawn, honest! Look! S'him. Honest! Look! Oh! Honest! S'him!' she's squealing – 'Look!'

Dawn's bewildered – 'Eh? Wit? Who? Wit ye talkin aboot? Who? Where? Ye talkin aboot? Angie! Who?' she shouts.

Johnny strolls down the steps – 'Hauw! Wi gaun fura joint?' he smiles.

Dawn can't believe her eyes. Johnny's free. He has walked. They jump up and rush him – 'Oh Johnny! Johnny! Wit the fuck's happened? How did ye get oot? Did they let ye oot? Oh Johnny! Johnny! Johnny!' they squeal.

Johnny's grinning broadly – 'PF's release. Aye, honest! Came in an telt me earlier a wis tae go tae the surgery. Next thing am oan ma way o'er here. Walked. Here. Yer noa gonny believe this. Mind that copper?'

They're roaring and laughing – 'Whit? That fat bastard? Yer jokin, Johnny? Dun fur Barney?'

Johnny's shaking his head – 'Naw the Paki. Dun um fur that. Aw, al explain later when wi get up the road. How ye daen darlin?' he smiles.

Angie bows her head – 'Bran new. Told ye, dint a?' she says.

Johnny's puzzled – 'Eh? Witsat? Told me wit?'

Angie looks into his eyes – 'Ad visit ye.'

Blackhill cemetry looms up as they pass in the bus. Death is rarely far away. They've better things to do now. They pay no attention to the little figure standing at a freshly dug grave.

A black shawl covers the old woman's face. She sits down by the grave, talking. They don't hear her words.

'Well, Bernard. S'a nice day. Bit cauld. A goat masel that electric fire. Aye, son. Might huv a wee holiday wi the muney ye left. Yer an awful boy. Aye, eh. Hope yer behavin yerself. A miss ye singin, son. S'quiet noo. Sittin in the hoose masel. Aye, eh. Hope yer lookin efter yerself. Keepin yerself warm in the night, son. S'gettin cauld at night, eh. The electric fire makes a difference so it dis.'

Auld Bessie rearranges the flowers on the grave – 'S'better noo. Aye, eh. Well. Al jist get doon the road noo, son. V'got a pot a soup oan fur ye, jist incase. A keep ma eye open fur ye at the windae. Aye, eh. Well. See ye the morra, son. N'thanks fur thinkin aboot me, son. Gave the rest ey that money tae the priest. Said a nice prayer fur ye so ey did. Mind the cauld noo, son.'

Auld Bessie pulls the shawl up around her head – 'God luvs ye, son.'

Epilogue

SAUCHIEHALL STREET, GLASGOW. August 1976. Rain is bouncing off the road. People try to dodge humid traffic. Cars deliberately drag through puddles to flood them with the filthy hot rain. The three men standing in the doorway are drenched by a shower of muddy water.

'BASTARD! DIDYE SEE THAT CUNT? EY FUCKIN MEANT IT!'

The eldest of the group steps out from behind the other two bodies.

'Aye, eh. Summer. Never rains but it pours.' He hands his jacket to the younger of the two men.

'Okay, Peter, haud this. Here they come. Thur jist crossin o'er. See thum? S'they two there wi the hair. Lookit thum, eh. Like two ey the apostles.'

Pretending to lock the door of the car parked at the kerb, he throws the bunch of keys to the other associate.

'Right, Kevin. You jist staun here. Noo jist let thum look in the boot, but nae touchin the stuff, okay? This'll be the best stuff they ever smoked, eh,' he sniggers.

Kevin, leaning against the car, scowls. Peter holds the jacket over his shoulder.

'On ye go.'

Everything is ready

Peter spits a goggle into a puddle – 'Fuckin longhairs,' he mutters.

The older man steps out, whispering out the side of his face – 'Here we go. Right. In an oot. Canny go wrang.'